the Summer of

of

BaD
IDeas

the Summer of BaD IDeas

Kiera Stewart

HARPER
An Imprint of HarperCollinsPublishers

First Edition

With love for Ron Bucknam, who has flown planes, sailed ships, swum with sharks, slept among scorpions, and raised a couple of kids, including me

Chapter 1

Kingdom, Phylum, Class, Order, Family

Twigs snap under the sure step of my boots. The sun strains through the clustered branches above, beaming rays of light into the eerie coolness of the forest air. Beneath me, unseen creatures rustle and slither and scatter; around us, they chirp and coo and call out.

I am hiking through the woods with Taylor, and I am not afraid.

No, wait. I'm not just hiking. I am *leading* Taylor on a summer adventure through the wild, and we're making our way toward a lake. A murky lake. In which I will swim, even though you can't see the bottom. A murky lake into which

I will *dive*. Swan dive! Yes, that's even better. Taylor will cheer me on as I prepare for the big leap, and I won't feel scared at all. Not even a tiny bit—

The minivan screeches to a stop. There is a collective *thwack* of five seat belts suddenly snapping into action. I am physically yanked back into the unwelcome reality that I am in the sweltering state of Florida, and for the last few days, I have been confined to a vehicle with my parents and eight-year-old twin siblings. I am no adventurer; there is nothing exciting or fun or fearless about me. I'm a crumb-covered kid with only a dream, and very little free will to do anything about it.

"Sorry about that, fam," my dad says. "But what the *dangle*?" He is staring at something in the road.

"Well, this means we're almost there," my mom says with a flustered sigh. I've noticed that the closer we get to her childhood home, the stranger she's acting.

"Is that a dog?" Beatrice squints excitedly from the seat behind me. She lost her glasses in one of the Carolinas, so now she and Henry are sharing his.

But it's not a dog. It's a dinosaur. A huge, bright-green monster sort of thing with a row of thorns along its neck. The twins *ooh* and *ah* behind me, passing Henry's glasses back and forth.

"Oh. That's Barbara," my mom says. "She's an iguana."

"Okay, who wants to classify it?" my dad, the biologist, asks.

"*Common green iguana!*" Henry shouts, his words stabbing into my ear. "Phylum—Chordata. Class—Reptilia. Order—"

"Kingdom—animalia! You forgot kingdom," Beatrice corrects him.

"I left it out. Everyone already knows *that*."

Henry reaches for his video camera with one hand; with the other, he grabs for the side-door handle. But, having forgotten to unbuckle his seat belt, he falls awkwardly between his seat and the door, camera rolling.

Snap. My mom has activated the child lock on the side door. "Edith, can you—"

"I'm helping, I'm helping," I say as I pull Henry back into his seat. IQ-wise, the twins are technically geniuses, but common-sense-wise, it's a different story. It's not unusual for me to have to help them out of ridiculous situations. Once, while pretending to be an armadillo, Beatrice got her head wedged in the back of her chair. And there was the time that Henry got stuck in the washer over an argument about centripetal versus centrifugal force.

My mom reaches over my dad in the driver's seat and starts honking the horn. "Move, Barbara! *Move!*" The iguana slowly slinks into the tall grass at the side of the road, and we start moving again. "Petunia did always let her wander."

"Um, *Mom*?" I ask.

"It's the next left," she says to my dad, sitting back in her seat as if there's nothing weird about any of this.

"Mom!"

"Yes, honey. What?" my mom asks, a little impatiently.

"Uh, what the heck? Is going on?" I ask as we turn into a driveway, which is just a *looong* path of gravel.

"I know, it's a little surprising. Barbara has to be more than twenty years old. She always liked roaming. Petunia didn't want to keep her in a cage—she thought it would 'ruin the iguana's spirit,'" she says, making air quotes. "Now, that alligator of hers was a different story."

"Alligator?" Henry, Beatrice, and I ask in unison, but with completely different tones. Disbelieving, intrigued, and absolutely terrified. Respectively.

"His name was Louis," my mom says. "He hardly had any teeth. She fed him cat food. And he had to be kept in a caged area—for his own protection."

My dad smiles and shakes his head. "Petunia and her reptiles."

"Mom?" My skin starts to itch. I'm beginning to feel cold even though it's about a hundred degrees outside. "You didn't exactly say Petunia had reptiles. You said *animals*. That

Petunia was really into her *animals*."

"She was. She loved animals. Particularly reptiles. But, obviously, it's been a while since I've been here, so I'm not really sure what to expect."

"What about"—I brace myself for the answer—"snakes?"

"Edith's afraid of snakes," Beatrice says.

I cringe. "I'm not *afraid*," I try to argue. "I just don't *like* them. I also don't like worms, but that doesn't mean I'm afraid of them."

"If you don't like worms, why did you want to go camping, then?" Henry asks. "You were going to sleep in a tent on the ground. Worms live in the ground."

"It doesn't matter. *Mom* wasn't going to let me go anyway," I say pointedly.

He's talking about Sophi Angelo's summer kickoff party—THE summer kickoff party. A weekend camping trip to Wompatuck State Park. My best friend, Taylor, was the one officially invited, but she talked Sophi into inviting me. Going on that trip could have meant that I'd still have a best friend in the fall, when we start middle school. Or at least I'd have a shot.

"Well, I'm sorry, Edith, but Sophi's parents were going to be in an RV on the other side of the campground," my mom says. "I just wasn't comfortable with it. A group of twelve-year-olds—"

"Almost thirteen!" I say.

"But still, *twelve*-year-olds should be supervised a lot more closely. They should *not* be wandering around a campground on their own all weekend. It's too risky. The chance of something happening is pretty high."

"Yeah, something *fun*," I grumble. Okay, so maybe my mom's shoulds and shouldn'ts saved me from some possible snake encounters. And Sophi *was* talking about swimming in the lake *at night*. And having a campfire! *And* sneaking off to spy on some ninth-grade boys. The sad truth is that all of it scares me. I'd probably have spent the weekend curled up in the corner of a tent.

"And anyway, honey, I told you you could have your own sleepover."

Right. Well. It's no surprise that Taylor chose the popular Sophi Angelo and her big weekend camping party over spending another *boring* night at my house. But what *is* a surprise, at least to me, is that I've barely heard from her since.

Sleepovers—and stories—are something that Taylor and I have had a lot of, at least until recently. Taylor has a serious food allergy, and when we first met in fourth grade, her mother knew she'd be safe at our house with my mom in charge. And *my* mom knew that we'd be well supervised at Taylor's house. And it turned out we had a lot in common, mainly books. Reading good ones and writing bad ones. As wannabe authors, we've attempted five together, mysteries that all remain, sadly, unfinished and unsolved. But lately, Taylor's mom has been letting her do more things that used to be off-limits—parties, social events, weekend camping trips! Now that Taylor seems to have more choice about who she hangs out with, she seems to be choosing less of me.

Thankfully, Beatrice changes the subject. "So *are* there snakes here, Mom?" she asks, in an annoyingly hopeful tone.

"*Well . . . ,*" my mom says, in this high-pitched singsongy way that comes across a little apologetic. Her eyes catch mine in the rearview mirror.

Oh, no.

"She used to have some. If there are any snakes still around—"

If. Which, in this case, you don't have to be a genius to figure out means YES THERE ARE MANY SNAKES AROUND, CAN'T YOU SEE ALL THE GREAT HIDING PLACES IN THE OVERGROWN GRASS AND HANGING TREE LIMBS, YOU FOOL YOU.

"—we should all remember, the vast majority of snakes aren't harmful to humans. If you don't bother them, they won't bother you," my mom says, as if it's just a matter of knowledge and/or memory.

"Yeah," Henry says. "More people die each year from bee stings than snakebites."

"Errrrrr." Beatrice makes a loud buzzing sound and frantically presses an imaginary button in front of her. "Misleading statistic! More people are actually *allergic* to bee stings than snakebites. They die of *allergies.*"

My dad clears his throat. "Edith, Petunia kept her snakes in an enclosure, but I'll take a good look around once we get settled in and make sure everything is nice and secure."

I know my dad thinks it's his fault that I *really* don't like snakes. I think he's been feeling guilty about it for almost six years now, since he took me to the snake habitat at the zoo.

"You shouldn't be afraid, Edith," Beatrice says again.

"I'm *not*!" I say, despite the prickle of goose bumps down my arms and the heat of shame across my face.

The gravel road curves, and my grandmother's house comes into view. It's like one of those plantation homes you'd see in an old black-and-white movie—a huge two-story with double balconies, rounded at the front and surrounded by a large porch and imposing columns. It's the kind of house that makes you want to sit up a little straighter. Even though it looks a little dusty and dingy, and mind-blowingly old, my mouth falls open a little.

"Wow," I say. Compared to our split-level in the Boston suburbs, it's practically a mansion. "You grew up here?" I ask my mom.

"Yeah." Her voice is soft as she studies the house through

the car window. She turns to my dad. "I just always thought that someday she'd meet the children." She shakes her head. "I mean, all the crazy risks she took—swimming with sharks and scuba diving and those self-guided trips to the Everglades—who would have thought?"

My dad reaches over and squeezes her shoulder. "No one expected it."

It is a little ironic. My grandmother did a lot of dangerous things in her life—and survived. But ten days ago, she died from a sudden heart attack, just sleeping peacefully in her bed.

After what feels like an unofficial moment of silence, my dad clears his throat. "Now, kids," he says, looking up at the house. "This is what they call Greek revival. It was a popular building style before the Civil War. That porch is called a portico, and the window above the door is a transom." Another teaching moment, as almost everything is in our family. Thankfully, this is slightly more pleasant than the anatomy lesson we had over some skunk roadkill in South Carolina.

The house looks still and quiet, even a little abandoned.

"What time did A.J. say they'd be here, Hannah?" my dad asks.

My uncle, A.J.—my mom's younger brother—and my cousin Rae will be spending these next two weeks cleaning out the house with us. I've never met them—nor have I met Petunia, nor my grandfather, who died before I was born. Apparently I have a family full of strangers. Still, I'm pretty sure I know what to expect. I've seen a couple of Rae's school portraits over the years—the trademark glasses, the much-needed braces, the strained smile. Her mother is Korean American, so even though Rae's skin tone is different than mine, there's apparently no escaping the very dominant dork gene that runs in our family like an Olympic track star.

"He just said early." My mom looks at her watch. "It's after four now, though. Maybe their plane was late."

I'm glad to hear it. After being cooped up in the car with my parents and the twins for three full days, the last thing I need now is even *more* family around me. The child lock unsnaps, and I slide open the side door and step out. The second I stand up, I am reminded of the giant iced tea I guzzled about a hundred miles back.

"Mom, where's the bathroom?" I ask.

"Oh, let's get these suitcases out of the car and then I'll show you, honey." She pulls on a suitcase that seems stuck. My dad tries to wrestle it free.

"I can go on my *own*, Mom."

"Well, of course you can, Edith, but I don't know the condition of the house. My mother wasn't much of a house-keeper. I'd rather—"

"Mom? Please. I think I can handle it."

She exhales. "Okay, Edith, listen. The key's probably right under the doormat. The bathroom's in the back of the house. You'll have to go down the front hall and through the kitchen." She reaches for another suitcase. "But be *careful*."

The wooden porch steps groan under my feet. I peel up the doormat, but there's no key. I try the knob. It turns, unlocked. I push open the heavy door and step inside.

And stop.

Going into my grandmother's house is like entering someone's bad dream. So far, I'm not a fan of Florida—being anywhere in this state is like getting trapped in your P.E. teacher's armpit after an aggressive game of dodgeball—but at least outside, there's sun, and bright colors, and a breeze. And, let's be honest, probably poisonous snakes. With fangs. But inside this house, the dark air feels thick and heavy, like it's closing in on me. Dust swirls through the air like plankton in water.

I blink and my eyes adjust. A wide, sweeping staircase spirals into the foyer. It looks grand but also reminiscent of things like ghosts. Which I don't believe in, I remind myself. I look down the long hall, toward the daylight coming through the kitchen window. It seems a long way away.

I feel that too-familiar tingle of fear and begin to turn around to wait outside for my mom after all. But I stop myself.

Maybe it's time for a new Edith. A braver Edith. A gutsier one. An Edith who wouldn't be hiding in a tent while other people are swimming at night. Having campfires. Meeting up with boys.

An Edith who *definitely* wouldn't be waiting for her mother to take her to the bathroom.

So I ignore the goose bumps, and the bad smells, and the reasons why not, and dare myself to take another step into the dark house.

Chapter 2

Stuffed

I am almost into the main hall when I hear something move.

I look to the left and freeze. At the entry to a cluttered room with soaring ceilings, a large gray-and-black dog stands at attention, staring at me. *Gutsy Edith*, I remind myself. My heart races. "Nice boy?" I ask slowly.

But his big blue eyes don't even blink. The dog seems unnaturally still. I notice he's standing on a small wooden platform.

"His name's Albert," I hear, and I startle, jump, and gasp at the same time, so it's sort of like performing a dancing snort.

"He's stuffed. You know—taxidermy. Petunia liked that kind of thing."

My eyes scan over rows and rows of books, a desk, a wooden lamp carved into the shape of a coiled snake. Then I see her—a girl, curled up on a faded floral-print couch in the corner of the large room. She pushes herself up to a seated position, tucks her long black hair behind her ear, and smiles a little. I'm not sure if she's being friendly or just trying not to laugh at me.

"Sorry to scare you," she says. "Guess it's a good thing that stuffed alligator isn't around."

Yes, good thing indeed. I smile sheepishly back and try to explain myself. "Oh, no, I wasn't—uh, *scared*. I just didn't know anyone was in the house."

"My dad went into town to get some groceries, but I was hoping to FaceTime my friends. No luck. The signal really sucks." She stretches her arms up. "I guess I fell asleep."

I squint through my glasses. She looks familiar. And then it hits me. I've seen this girl before. I've watched her steal a Rocket Pocket Pastry Puff from her "older brother." I've seen her dance around with a cartoon Pollo Mio chicken. I am standing about fifteen feet in front of a celebrity.

"Uh . . . ," I sort of stammer. "You're the girl in those commercials."

"Oh." She laughs. "Those are so embarrassing. My dad

didn't write about those in the Christmas letter, did he?"

Dad? Christmas letter? Could this be—?

I stare at her, noticing everything from her shiny hair to her hot-pink flip-flops. There's no sign of braces, but I guess those can come off. And could she be wearing contacts? Yes. *Yes,* she could.

This girl is . . . "*You're* Rae?" I hear myself ask.

We may be close to the same age and share about twelve and half percent of our genes, but at the moment, I'm having trouble figuring out which genes those are. We're both wearing shorts and T-shirts, but compared to her, I look like a poorly wrapped UPS package. Her hair is glossy and flowing, while mine is like a scribble with a tan crayon. Her eyes are golden brown, mine are tombstone gray. Maybe there's some similarity in our left pinkie toes.

"Yeah," she says slowly. "And you're Edith, right?"

I nod. "You just look so different from your school pictures."

She tucks her chin. "From when? Fourth grade? Yuck. I looked like such a dweeb with those huge glasses—"

Her words stop. My own glasses now seem to be under some sort of bright spotlight. They feel suddenly massive, like those oversized glasses people sometimes wear as a joke. I push them up the bridge of my nose and look away.

"Never mind, I just mean . . . burn those pictures when

you get back, okay, Edith? Burn them." She gives me an awkward smile. "Well, welcome, I guess. I've been here all day. Our flight got in at the butt crack of dawn."

A nervous sensation bubbles up in my throat. It starts as a laugh, but by the time it reaches my mouth it's become a shriek. I basically turn into a human fire alarm.

Because on a plaque on the wall, right above the couch where my cousin is sitting, is a five-foot-long snake, spotted like a leopard and shaped into a S. My eyes squeeze shut, my hands are like claws attached to my head, and over my scream, I hear her ask, "Oh, this?"

My scream stops. My eyes open. She is pointing to the viper.

"Uh, yeah?" I say.

"He's stuffed too. Herbie," she says. "I think he was her favorite."

The nerves ping throughout my body. My eardrums reopen. "She had a favorite *viper*?"

"No, Herbie was a ball python." She pauses for a second, sighs, and says, "There's more snakes out back, in enclosures. Rat snakes."

I wonder if I look anything like I feel. I guess I do, because she looks at me a little strangely and asks, "You okay? You're not afraid of snakes, are you?"

I try to make myself laugh. "No, I mean, what's there to

be afraid of?" And then I find myself *actually quoting Henry.* "More people die from bee stings than snakebites."

"Oh, *phew,*" she says, wiping imaginary sweat from her forehead. "'Cause, wow—that would get old really fast. They're everywhere down here!" And she laughs. Like a *breeze.*

I try the breeze-laugh thing too, but I sound more like an electric can opener. But she's too busy joking around and reaching up and PUTTING HER FINGERS IN THE SNAKE'S MOUTH to notice.

"So," I say, trying to collect myself, "have you been here before?"

"Just a couple times. Mostly she came out to visit us. She liked the surfing in California. You ever been surfing?"

"Me? No, never!" The words blurt out way too fast. No wonder Taylor is probably off cliff diving and mountain climbing and god knows what else with Sophi Angelo. "I mean, it's because of my mom. She would never let me do anything like that, but you know, I would."

"Oh. I don't really have one of those *mom* moms," Rae says.

I suddenly remember that Rae's mom doesn't live with her. Everything I say seems to be uncomfortably wrong. Still, I keep talking. "Also we live near the northeast coast and our waves just—well, there's probably not enough wind velocity."

Wind velocity. *What?*

I need to stop talking as soon as possible. But what I start to do is laugh. And it comes out in a weird, gurgly, snorty sound, like a pig rooting around in its trough. *Snort, wheeze, gurgle, chortle, snort.* Very unfortunately, this happens sometimes when I get extremely nervous. Especially when I'm around someone I like.

I try to hold my breath, but it bursts through once again.

"You've got the funniest laugh," Rae says. She looks entertained, at least. "That *is* a laugh, right?"

For once, I'm glad to hear my mom calling me from outside. "Well, I should—" *Snort.* I point to the front door.

"Okay, I'll come with you." Rae pops up off the couch, and somehow I end up following her to the front door.

Outside, my family is sorting through the luggage. The twins have been assigned to collecting the trash in the van.

"Did you find the bathroom?" my mom asks without looking up at me.

"Well, no. But I *did* find—" The words *your niece* sound, ironically, too familiar. So I just say, "Rae."

"Hi," Rae says. "Aunt Hannah?"

My mom smiles big. She steps toward Rae and pauses. For a second I wonder if my mom will do something completely out of character and hug this near-stranger. But she doesn't. Instead, she takes Rae's hand into her own and shakes it with

18

a little extra gusto. "Dr. Hannah Posey-Preston," she says, like she's at a statistics convention and not her own childhood home. "It's so nice to meet you."

My dad embarrasses me in an altogether different way. He does this little circle-like wave in front of his head and *bows*. "Pleased to make your acquaintance, Miss Rae. I am Walter Posey-Preston, aka Uncle Walt."

"Oh, hi," Rae says with a bewildered giggle.

"Allow me to introduce the twins," my dad says, in his mock-formal attempt at humor. "Beatrice, the girl child, of course, and Henry, the boy."

"Awesome to meet you guys," Rae says to them.

"Pleased to meet you," Henry says, like he's eighty years old, not just eight.

"So, twins, huh?" Rae asks, sizing up the two inches of height Beatrice has on Henry, and Beatrice's brown hair versus Henry's white-blond. The glasses are back on Beatrice.

"We're dizygotic," Henry answers, shrugging.

Rae tries to repeat it—with a question mark—but stumbles over the pronunciation.

"It just means fraternal twins," I interpret.

"Yeah, we came from different eggs," Henry adds, igniting within me an impulse to flee.

But Rae gives me a secret smile, as if releasing me from the guilt of association. "They're a*dorable*," she says.

"Mom, she said the A-word!" Beatrice announces.

"Beatrice, it's *fine*." My mom smiles apologetically at Rae. "Really, it's fine."

"That word makes us feel trivialized," Henry tells Rae.

"Henry!" my mom softly scolds him. To Rae, she says, "I'm so sorry, they're sometimes a little sensitive. . . ."

Which clearly translates into *freakishly weird*, but I'm too mortified to speak, let alone attempt to interpret again.

"I'm . . . sorry, I guess?" Rae says. "Cute, then? Can I say *cute*?"

The twins take a communal gasp.

"Even worse," Henry says.

"Now, *twins*," my dad says. "Rae is trying to say something nice to you. It's a compliment. Just say thank you."

The twins mumble their thanks, and my mom turns to Rae again, looking a little defeated. "I'm really so sorry, Rae. They haven't exactly mastered the concept of *tact*."

Would it really be too much to ask to have my family, just once, act like normal people? I'm starting to feel like I did when I was nine and went to Wurstland with Taylor. We went in the spinning sausage ride, and the minute I got strapped in, I realized I wanted off. I *needed* off. I cried and screamed until they stopped the ride just to get me out of there.

But let's face it. No one's going to rescue me from this spinning sausage of a summer.

My dad hands me a huge duffel bag to take inside. Rae grabs a small suitcase, and the two of us head up the porch steps and set the luggage down inside the foyer. After finally getting that bathroom break, I start back outside, but Rae says, "Hey, let's go upstairs. I want to show you something."

I know my parents are expecting me to help unpack. I know the twins want me to help lug their stuff into the house. "Oh, but, I should—" The words come out like a reflex. I'm so used to those words. *I should* keep an eye on the twins. *I should* make good choices. *I should* follow the rules. I *should* be sensible. Careful. Smart. Safe. I should, I should, I *should*.

She smiles at me. "Oh, come on, cousin."

I like the idea of being related to someone like her. She wouldn't be curled up in the tent while her friends went swimming in the lake at night. She'd be the first to dive in.

So I shut the shoulds up and follow my cousin up the stairs.

Chapter 3

Good Ideas

"*Ta-da!*"

Rae spreads her arms and twirls around. We're in an untidy and dust-coated upstairs room at the back of the house. An old desk is covered with stuff—bills, mail, an old calendar, yellowed newspapers. A purple suitcase, half emptied, lies open on the brass bed, like she's already started to unpack. Across the room is a worn olive-green couch.

Rae's obviously comfortable here, but it feels a little strange to me to be standing in a room that's been so lived in, when I don't really know the person who did the living in it.

"So." She throws her arms out wide. "What do you think?"

"About this room?"

"Yeah."

I want to say the right thing, I do. My problem is that I don't know what that is. Having spent enough time on the sidelines watching popular girls interact, I know that answering these kinds of questions truthfully sometimes has a negative effect. So I stand there like a dummy, with a left-over smile that's starting to make my face hurt.

"Okay," she says, "I know. It's a little messy, but trust me, it's the best room in the house."

I look around and notice the strange things covering the surfaces. An assortment of animal figurines dot the shelves—a thick metal lizard, a replica of an iguana, a cobra head carved out of quartz. A few framed photos perch on a bookshelf. A snapshot of two toddlers—my mom and Uncle A.J, probably—stands next to a photo of an alligator. And an old black-and-white image of a teenage girl, holding a snake across her forearms. A thick snake.

"Oh, classic photo," Rae says. "That's Petunia with her first pet snake."

For a second, I'm confused. This shy smile doesn't seem to belong to the fearless grandmother I've heard about. But it does look familiar—her smile looks a little like mine.

I walk over to the shelf to get a better look at the young Petunia, but when I pick up the picture, a hook on the back of the frame swings open. Out falls a folded piece of paper—lined and hole punched, like the paper we use in school. It's brittle with age, and I carefully unfold it, trying to keep it from cracking apart.

"What is it?" Rae asks.

"It's some kind of list," I say, looking it over. The items are written in loopy cursive, in different inks—a graying black, a faded blue. I flatten it out on the desk, and we look at it together.

Petunia's Good Ideas for Summertime, 1962
Caution: Not for the Fainthearted!!!
1. Catch a snake bare-handed.
2. Discover hidden treasures.
3. Dance in the hurricane.
4. Master flirting.
5. Wish upon a shooting star.
6. Write something scary.
7. Cross Corkscrew Swamp under a FULL MOON.
8. Hug the person you least want to.
9. Kiss the charmer.
10.

The last item on the list is blank. "Looks like she had a busy summer—too busy to complete the list," I say.

"Sounds like Petunia. She was always off on some kind of adventure," Rae says, looking amused.

I try to sound more curious than horrified at the first item on the list. "I wonder why she wanted to catch a snake in the first place."

"Yeah, too bad we can't ask her now. The only thing we *do* know is that she's got a bunch of them out back."

Thanks for the reminder. I make myself smile. It takes real effort.

"'Discover hidden treasures,'" Rae reads from the list. "I know what I'd do if I found any. I'd sell it all and buy us a real summer vacation!"

We laugh, and I glance back at the piece of paper. "'Dance in the hurricane'! That sounds kind of crazy."

Rae shrugs. "I don't know what that's like. We don't really have hurricanes in California."

"Well, it would be really dangerous. Even Category One hurricanes have winds over seventy miles an hour—that can rip a roof off a house. If it's a Category Five, winds are like a hundred and fifty miles an hour! That's why they evacuate coastal areas when—" *Ugh.* I stop myself before I start rattling off advice on flashlights and bottled water. It's not like Rae has signed up for a safety seminar!

She looks at me like she thinks I'm slightly insane. Distraction seems to be the only defense. I read another item off the list. "'Master flirting.'" I crinkle my nose. "It's a little weird to think of your grandmother in that way."

"Not if you knew her. I bet she was a huge flirt when she was young." Rae scans her finger down to the last item on the list and glances up with a wry grin. "'Kiss the charmer,' in case you need proof of that."

It embarrasses me to even think about it. I look at the list. "'Wish upon a shooting star.' I wonder what she wished for."

But something else has Rae's attention. "'Write something scary.'"

It makes me miss Taylor all over again. I think about our latest unfinished writing attempt—a story we titled "The Year I Was Gina." Will we ever finish one of our stories now?

"How about this for something scary?" Rae mimics writing in the air with her pointer finger as she speaks. "Once upon a time there were two girls. Cousins. One day, their parents told them, 'Guess what? You're going to have to give up two weeks of your summer and spend it in an old house in Florida, where you will scrub and clean and fix things and probably sweat to death before you can escape.'" She laughs. "Because that sounds pretty scary to me."

Meeting Rae has made the idea of spending two weeks here almost bearable, but her joke makes it seem like she doesn't feel the same. I force that smile again. "Yeah. Scary."

"Well, okay, not scary, exactly. But *sooo* boring."

There's that word again.

It was the last day of school, just a few days before Sophi's camping trip. Taylor had already been invited, and I was still hoping to be. I was in the car with my dad and the twins; the carpool line was inching forward. Glancing in the side mirror from the passenger's seat, I saw Taylor and Sophi walking down the sidewalk in our direction, clueless to the fact that I was within earshot. I could hear them chatting about the trip.

Then I heard Taylor say, "What about Edith? Weren't you going to invite her?"

Sophi's response felt like a slap to me. "Edith's no fun."

And Taylor said something I couldn't hear, and then laughed. Actually *laughed*.

"Seriously, Taylor," Sophi said. "Don't you think she's boring?"

But it was Taylor's next words that were daggers in my heart. She said, "Well, yeah, but just invite her anyway. Her mom probably won't let her go."

My soul sank as I thought about all the fun I thought we'd had over our two years together. Not just writing, but the Yoda sodas (allergy friendly). Mad Libs. Chess club. Trivia with the supertwins—even they seemed tolerable around her. I thought she understood me and my weird family, as I understood hers, and now she was being lured away because it was all so *boring*.

"Hey, you okay?" Rae asks me now.

"Oh, I'm fine," I say, trying to pull myself out of my head. I pick up the photo again. Even though the idea of holding a snake makes me want to run off and curl into a tight little ball, I can't stop looking at the photo. *This* is the person I never got to know.

Rae notices me staring at the picture. "Petunia used to say, 'Do something every day that scares the daylights out of you.'"

I think about that, and the fact that she's holding a snake—her first snake—in the photo. Did it once scare the daylights out of her? I scan the other items on her list of ideas: cross Corkscrew Swamp under a full moon; hug the person you least want to. Did these things once scare her?

Then Rae lifts her chin, furrows her brow, and says, in a dramatic voice, "Carpe diem. Seize the day. Make your life"—she closes her eyes—"*extraordinary.*"

"Was that one of her sayings too?"

"No." She smiles. "It's what *I* say."

I look at my cousin. My cool California cousin. My seize-the-day cousin. "I like that," I say.

The door opens and Beatrice barges in. "It's almost time for dinner."

"Okay, we'll be right there," I say.

"Rae's dad is here."

"Fine, we're coming," Rae says.

"We have a dog," Beatrice says. "Odysseus."

"Oh, that's Albert," I say. "But I'll be—"

"His name's Odysseus *now*," she declares.

"All right. Now go, please."

But Beatrice still doesn't budge. "Is this where you're going to sleep?" she asks.

"Beatrice, can you please just— We'll be down in a minute."

When she leaves, *finally*, Rae says, "So, are you going to? Sleep in here, I mean? You can have the couch. It'll be fun."

I hesitate. "Are you sure?"

"Yeah, Edie, I'm sure. When we leave here in a couple weeks, I'm going straight to Shakespeare camp. Then I'll have *three* roommates. So I should probably get used to sharing a room."

I'm struck—not just because she's basically inviting me to move in with her, but because she's just called me Edie. I've always wanted to be an Edie, but every time I've tried to launch a "call me Edie" campaign, it's been like trying to change an ocean tide, and I end up stuck with the stodgy-sounding Edith. But now, in just a matter of two seconds, she's made me feel twenty times cooler.

"Okay, sure," I say, trying not to smile too big.

The door opens again. My mom pokes her head in. "Downstairs in five minutes, okay, girls? We're going out to eat."

"Why are we eating so early?" I ask.

"Well," she says, "I'd like to make sure we have time to talk."

There's something weird about the very careful way she's speaking, but I just say, "Fine." When she leaves, I say to Rae, "Sorry about that. Her bursting in here and all."

She shrugs. "No worries. What do you think she wants to talk about?"

But before I can answer—safety rules, of course, knowing my mom; might as well brace Rae for it—we're summoned downstairs, this time by my dad. "Eeeee-dith!" He sort of sings it. "We're ready to blow this taco stand!"

Rae laughs.

I let out an exasperated sigh. "We're coming!" I call down.

We close the door to *our* room behind us—it feels good to already have something of ours—and head downstairs to our waiting families. I brace myself for whatever lies ahead.

Chapter 4

Endangered

We are at the BEST Diner in Town. That's not a description; it's the name of the place. It shouts at us in neon—the word *best* in wide, all-cap letters on top, *Diner in Town* underneath.

And, in Pinne, Florida, the BEST Diner in Town is also the ONLY Diner in Town. The parking lot is pretty empty except for a few old cars, including a yellow Corvette with a racing stripe, which turns out to belong to the waitress-slash-owner, Dani—an old acquaintance of the family. From a distance, her heavy face and her low ponytail of fading red hair make her appear old, but when she sees us and gives us a welcoming smile, she seems to become decades younger.

There's a little catching up, and some condolences. "Sorry about your mom," Dani says. "I suppose she's at peace."

"Yeah, that's probably the last place she wants to be," Uncle A.J. jokes, and the three of them share a laugh, although my mom's is more like a little whimper.

It feels strange to order drinks and burgers after that, but that's what most of us do. My uncle orders a basket of fried pickles for the table, even though my mom shoots him a disapproving look. My mom tries to get away with a salad, but Dani won't allow it.

"A salad? Well, you're going to waste away with just a salad. How about I make it burgers all around? Listen to me. You got to keep your strength up in times like this."

"Times like what?" Beatrice asks.

"Times of grief," Dani explains. Then she asks our parents, "Speaking of, I hear there's not going to be a funeral?"

Uncle A.J. speaks. "Petunia didn't want a funeral. She just wanted—"

"She gets to be part of a coral reef!" Henry interrupts, just bursting with excitement.

"She wanted her ashes donated to the Neptune Memorial Reef. They have a man-made coral reef off the coast of Miami," Uncle A.J. explains.

"That certainly sounds like our Petunia," Dani says, and sighs. "I sure do miss having her around."

"Can I please have my ginger ale?" Henry asks Dani.

My parents both visibly cringe, and my dad starts to apologize for Henry's tactlessness, but Dani just shoos it away. "It's okay—I'm sure you're all thirsty." She goes off to get our drinks.

My mom turns to Rae, changing the subject. "So, Rae, tell me about school. Are you excited about starting seventh grade in the fall?"

"I'm not actually going into a grade, Aunt Hannah," Rae answers. "I'm going into *indigo*."

Uncle A.J. explains, "Rae goes to an arts school. She's studying theater and film."

"We're not limited to numbers," Rae adds.

"There's nothing limiting about numbers," Henry says. "Have you ever heard of infinity?"

"Henry," my mom gently scolds.

Uncle A.J. smiles at me. He's got that kind of smile that makes you feel like you're in on some private joke with him.

"How about you all?" Uncle A.J asks. "Edith, you're headed to a new school, aren't you?"

My mom answers. "Yes, Edith will be starting middle school—"

Yeah. Where she will have no friends.

"—and the twins go to the science-and-tech school. Henry's concentration is biology—"

33

"And documentary production," Henry adds.

"Yes," my mom says. "And Beatrice is studying zoology."

"Animal science," Beatrice says.

Uncle A.J. nods. "Well, that's awesome, guys. Obviously, you're all really—"

I suck in a breath.

"—intelligent," he says. The twins look satisfied, and I exhale.

"You know what, Hannah?" Uncle A.J. says. "Know what I just realized? Edie's got Petunia's eyes. Same exact shade—that stormy gray. Don't you think, Hannah? She kind of takes after her grandmother."

The fact that he notices it makes me feel hopeful in some way.

"Takes after *Mom*?" my mother says, like it's a crazy suggestion. "I'm not sure I see it."

"Actually, Hannah, I can see it too," my dad says.

My mom glances over at me. "Just a tiny bit, I guess. Twins, why don't you tell Uncle A.J. and Rae about your summer project?"

"Oh, okay." Beatrice sits up in her seat. "We're working on a documentary—"

"—about *Vermivora bachmanii*," Henry interrupts.

My dad laughs gently. "You might want to explain what that is."

"Oh. It's Bachman's warbler," Henry says, like that makes any more sense to a normal person.

"It's a bird," Beatrice says.

But Henry jumps back in. "It's not just a bird, Beatrice! It's an *endangered* bird. The last confirmed sighting was 1988!"

I look at Rae and roll my (stormy-gray) eyes for her benefit.

Uncle A.J. asks, "You sure it won't be a wild goose chase?"

"No, it's a *warbler*, Uncle A.J. It's not a goose," Beatrice tells him.

"No, what I mean is, if it's that endangered, it's going to be hard to find in the first place, let alone film."

Henry and Beatrice become silent. My dad clears his throat. Amazingly, I don't think it's something that any of the geniuses have really ever considered.

Dani brings our burgers, and while we all start in on them, I notice my mom has barely touched hers. I guess my dad notices too, because he asks her if she's okay.

"Yeah, I'm fine. I just wish . . ." She shakes her head.

"I wish she was here with us now," Rae says.

"In her leopard-print pantsuit," my dad adds, smiling. My mom smiles a little too.

"With Herbie wrapped around her shoulders," Uncle A.J. says, and laughs. My parents and Rae do too. I try my best to laugh along, but all I can really do is smile stiffly, horrified at the very thought.

"Had to ask her to leave one time," Dani says as she refills our water glasses. "She was scaring off some Miami-bound tourists. The husband pitched a fit, and the wife nearly collapsed on the floor, just seeing this crazy old lady—well, I mean that in a good way—this crazy lady with a snake wrapped around her shoulders."

That gets another good laugh.

"What happened to the alligator she had?" Beatrice asks. "You know, the one with no teeth?"

"Oh, Louis," my mom says. "He died a while ago."

"Yeah, she had him taxidermied too," Uncle A.J. says. "Just like Herbie the snake. And Albert the dog."

"I think I miss Petunia," Beatrice says.

"You can't *miss* her," Henry says. "You can't miss someone you never met."

Beatrice scrunches her forehead. "Oh."

It may not be possible to actually miss someone you never met, but I do feel a little empty inside too. I reach out under the table and squeeze Beatrice's fingers.

My mom announces a sudden need to wash her hands and leaves the table. Rae starts talking about Petunia and her surfing trip out west, and I decide to follow my mother.

I find her drying her hands with a paper towel. "Oh, hi,

honey," she says, a smile flickering on her face.

"Are you . . . okay?" I ask.

"Yes, I'm fine. Just needed a moment." She looks over at me. "What's wrong?"

"Nothing, it's just . . ."

I hesitate. As much as she annoys me sometimes, I really don't like upsetting her.

"Honey, what?"

"Well, why didn't we ever get to meet Petunia?"

She starts to talk about how busy we've been. It's like she forgets that I was actually on all those educational vacations we've had time for—or, well, *eduvacations* if you're a Posey-Preston. The Smithsonian museums, the Library of Congress, the Hayden Planetarium.

I must have a look on my face that tells her I'm not exactly buying it, because she says, "Okay, I'll admit that my mother and I clashed quite a bit when I was growing up."

"How long have you been mad at her, then?"

"It's not that I'm mad at her, honey. It's just that we never did see eye to eye, and maybe because of that, I didn't make visiting her a priority."

"So why didn't you ever invite her to come visit us?"

"Oh, Edith . . ." She shakes her head. "I couldn't even have begun to imagine what she'd do if she came to visit. She'd have gone stir-crazy."

Right. I'm getting the picture. She was a zing. Like Rae. We, on the other hand, are thuds. All thuds.

"So we were too boring for her," I say.

"Oh, now, Edith. That's not what I mean. I *am* sorry that you never got to meet her." She smiles at me, but I don't smile back.

Then she takes a breath and says, *"Anyway."*

Anyway, at least in my mom's language, is the equivalent of "conversation over." It's like hitting a dead end. You can try to keep talking, but it'll quickly turn into a monologue. She throws away her paper towel, and I follow her back to the table.

"Everything okay?" my dad asks when we sit back down.

I shrug.

Dani comes over to ask if my mom meant to leave half her burger on her plate, or if she's still working on it.

"Oh, thanks, Dani. I'm full; you can take it. Guess I'm out of practice eating this kind of— I mean, food this good."

"You know, after a few weeks, you probably won't even miss your city food." Dani takes the plate and walks away.

"After a few weeks?" Rae scoffs. "Good thing we won't be here *that* long."

But my mom looks at my dad, and then over at my uncle, and says, "Well, A.J., Walt, I suppose we should tell them now."

"Tell us what?" Rae asks, looking first at her father, then at my parents.

My dad clears his throat and asks if anyone wants more pickles.

My uncle takes in a breath and lets it out slowly. It seems to take forever. "So Petunia's house is in a lot worse shape than we expected."

"Okay, so?" Rae says, her eyebrows pulling together.

"Well," says my mom, "Petunia's will requires that we all stay here together, fixing up the house and getting it ready to sell. We knew it was going to be a major cleanup, but it looks like the house needs quite a bit of repairing too."

Rae says, "But my dad knows how to fix everything, so—"

"Hey, sport, listen," Uncle A.J. says. "What we're trying to say is that it's going to take us a little longer than we thought."

"Um, how *much* longer?" I ask.

"We think it'll take about six weeks," my mom says. She takes a fried pickle.

"Six weeks?" Rae and I both exclaim. Two weeks was bad enough with Sophi Angelo trying to lure Taylor away from me! Now, six weeks? Six weeks apart will turn our friendship into toast!

My mom only gives us an apologetic tilt of her head.

But Rae sounds almost panicky. "Dad? You said *two* weeks! What about Shakespeare camp? Just send me back to California now. I can stay with Mom until camp starts."

"She's . . . not available," Uncle A.J. says, rubbing his neck.

"Yes, she is. She told me if I ever—" Rae's voice cracks.

"She can't, sport. She's got her hands full at the moment. I'm sorry."

"Can you believe this?" Rae turns to me. "We're stuck here all summer? This is a *disaster.*"

And it does sort of feel that way. Will Taylor be best friends with Sophi by the time we go home? Has Sophi already replaced me?

"Six weeks is good," Henry says, oblivious to the fact that it's bad timing for such a comment. I try to shut him up with a glare, but as usual, he's clueless. "We'll definitely find a Bachman's warbler in six weeks."

"Yeah, six weeks is a long time," Beatrice says happily. "That's enough time for three generations of fruit flies."

"It's enough time for a tadpole to change into a frog," Henry adds.

"*Errrrrr!*" Beatrice presses the imaginary button again. "*Wrong,* Henry. Maybe a tadpole to a toadlet, but not a tadpole to a *frog.*"

Henry ignores her. "In six weeks, a young snake can shed its skin three times."

"Snakes don't molt that much," Beatrice says.

"I said a young snake, Beatrice! They grow faster, so they shed their skin every couple of weeks!"

I get another creepy chill just thinking about snakes

again. My mind goes back to the photo of Petunia holding the snake, and Petunia's list of good ideas. But *good* ideas? Most of them seem like *bad* ideas. Reckless. Foolish. Unnecessary. Unsafe. I mean, sneaking into a hurricane? Crossing a swamp at night? *Kissing a charmer? CATCHING A SNAKE?*

And then I recognize the force behind these thoughts: the Posey-Preston practicality reflex, which automatically responds to the possibility of fun by questioning the purpose, plausibility, and peril of said opportunity. The reflex that will ensure that I'll stay nice and boring all my life, while people like Sophi steal away my best friend.

Beatrice turns to Uncle A.J. "We made a monarch butterfly in science. It only took thirty-eight days!"

"Wow. Sounds like a lot can happen in six weeks," Uncle A.J. says.

"You didn't *make* a monarch butterfly," Henry chides Beatrice. Then *he* turns to Uncle A.J. "Did you know that to become a butterfly, a caterpillar first has to digest itself? It becomes like a caterpillar soup—"

I suddenly know what I need to do.

Rae glances over at me, distraught. But when I look at her, I feel a flicker of hope. Because, yes, a lot can happen in six weeks.

A lot can change.

A lot.

Chapter 5

Oh, Boy

"Hey, Rae?"

"Hmm."

"You okay?"

"No."

We are in our room. In our beds. Okay, so mine's not really a bed—it's the old olive-colored couch. The lights are off, and it feels like Rae is in another world. I'm getting a little worried, because I need her to be in mine.

"I'm really sorry that we're going to be here all summer," I say.

"Yeah, same," she says.

"But maybe it won't be so bad."

"O, never shall sun that morrow see!"

"Um, Shakespeare?"

"Macbeth," she says, as if that explains it all.

I try again. "And sorry you can't stay with your mom."

"You mean my *momster*." Her voice sounds a little like it's breaking apart. The room gets quiet, and the darkness and silence start to magnify every sound—every rustle, every shift, every blink.

"I'm sure she, you know, misses you." I'm *not* sure, not really. But it's her mom, so she's got to miss her daughter, right? Doesn't that come with the territory?

"Well, whatever," she says, drawing in a breath. "Anyway, it's not *her* I'm going to miss. It's my besties."

I can't help but notice that it's a *plural*.

"Vivian, Alexia, Mattie. But mostly Leo. My boyfriend."

Oh. Her boyfriend. Of course she would have one.

"I can't believe I'm going to be stuck here all summer, sweating my skin off, while he's off rehearsing with someone else. This *sucks*." She picks up her phone, checks it, sighs again, and puts it back down. "No one seems to get it."

"Actually, I might," I say. "Get it, I mean."

"You do?"

"Yeah." I take in a breath and prepare to tell her about Taylor. How I'm possibly losing her to someone else, just like she's worried about losing this boyfriend. But—

43

"So you have a boyfriend too?" She seems to perk up at this idea.

"I, uh . . ." Somehow telling her that no, I meant my *only* friend—a singular bestie—doesn't seem like the thing to do. So instead I say, "Yeah."

Her voice brightens with interest. "What's his name?"

"Klaus," I blurt.

Oh, my. *Gosh.* What is coming out of my mouth? Who is this knee-jerk boyfriend? Oh, why couldn't I have invented a Drake, or a Max, or an Axel? It's like my subconscious is out to get me.

"Klaus?" she asks, in this baffled way. "Is he—?"

"German, he's German."

"*German?* How did you meet him?"

"Oh, I go to school with him."

"So is he like an exchange student?"

"Yes, uh-huh," I say.

Yikes. I imagine a blond boy in lederhosen, knees exposed. High white socks. A green hat with a feather. At this point I'd do anything to remove Klaus from either one of our imaginations, but even in the dark, I can see her smiling at me, like we're on the same team.

And I need her on my team, because with her, all things seem possible.

She flops back on her bed. "Oh my god, how are we going

to deal, Edie? I mean, the whole summer? I have no idea how we're going to get through it. *No idea.*"

Here's my chance. "I think I have an idea."

"You do? What?"

With Rae's help, maybe I can do all the things on the list, and I won't seem so boring. And maybe Sophi won't look so fun and exciting when I tell Taylor about my own adventures. In Florida. With my almost-famous cousin.

"Maybe . . ." I'm a little nervous about Rae's reaction. What if she thinks it's a terrible idea? "Maybe we should do the things on Petunia's list."

"Oh." Her tone sounds flat with disappointment. But then she says, "Hey, wasn't the first one something about a snake?"

"Yes." I swallow. "Fun, right?"

She seems to think about it. "Well, it's not Shakespeare camp, but I guess it's something postable."

"Postable?" I ask.

"You know, on Facebook, Instagram—that kind of thing."

"Oh, yeah," I say, like I know, though I don't. It's another rule of my mom's. No social media until I'm fourteen and my frontal cortex is more developed.

But Rae's starting to sound a teensy bit excited. Or at least amused. "Actually, that would be kind of cool. Can't you see it? A photo of me holding a snake?"

"Yeah." A nervous laugh sneaks out. "It would be."

"Oh my god, Edie! It would be *amazing*! I'd get so many likes!"

"Yeah, um—*so* cool!"

"Okay, Edie. Let's do it. At least they won't forget me back home," she says, although she seems far from being forgettable. Then she makes her voice rich and British-y, and says, "Though this be madness, yet there is method in it."

It sounds like Shakespeare again, but I don't dare question it.

"Edie, you're a genius."

Technically, I'm not. The twins, sure—but not me. I don't correct her. Because even if I don't get Shakespeare, I'm feeling pretty smart indeed.

Chapter 6

Wild Things

"So, how are we going to do this again?"

We're standing on the back porch, looking out toward the far part of the yard, where the snakes live in their hutlike enclosures. The morning sun shines like a spotlight on the gated cluster.

Rae tilts her head. "We've been through this three times already."

"I know, but . . . I just want to make sure it makes sense."

"Makes sense?" Rae asks, crinkling up her nose.

Ugh. I'm finding that Old Edith is pretty hard to shake. "I mean the plan," I say. "I just want to make sure *that* makes sense."

"Like we said a hundred times, we're going to go out there, release the snakes from the cage, and then catch them again. That's when the fun begins."

"So, we're catching *snakes*, as in plural?" I quietly swallow and try to keep my smile lifted, although item one on the list specifically says catch *a* snake. Which means *one*. Not hundreds!

She shrugs. "I think there are five of them out there. One snake is nice and all, but since I'm going to post this photo, the more the better, right?"

"Oh, yeah." And then I say something really dumb. "The more the merrier!"

"Good. Then let's just *do* it, not analyze it."

"Analyze what?" Beatrice says way too loudly, appearing at the back door. She stares at me with eyes that look a little bare. Henry stands behind her, holding his camera and blinking through the lenses. It's his turn with the glasses.

Rae shushes her. "Quiet. We're supposed to be cleaning out the study."

"Mom told us to come help you," Beatrice says.

"Why'd she do that?" I say under my breath.

"Because Henry was using the drill," Beatrice says. "He keeps thinking we can make a robot—"

"I already found a radio and a broken remote control," Henry says, "and Dad said we could have all the old electronics in the house—"

"But I keep telling him we need a micro servo, so it's not going to work," Beatrice explains, as if it makes any sense to Rae and me.

"Okay, well, thanks, guys, but we don't need your help right now," I say.

Henry starts to lift his camera. "What *are* you doing?"

"Nothing, okay? And don't even start—you're supposed to be filming birds, not us," I say. "Isn't Dad taking you to the nature reserve today?"

"Yes, later. He's helping Mom and Uncle A.J. with the *Isoptera* upstairs," he says smugly.

"You're allowed to just say *termites*," I tell him.

"So can we hang out with you?" Beatrice asks.

"Actually, Edie, let them," Rae says. "Henry can film us. That way we'll have our hands free to catch the snakes."

Henry and Beatrice both look at me with puzzled looks on their twin faces. Beatrice says, "But Edith's—"

"Twins," I say. "Look, do you want to come or not?"

"Yeah, but—" Beatrice tries.

"What is with you Posey-Prestons? Less talking, more doing," Rae says. "Well, come on. The day is just waiting to be seized!" She runs down the back-porch steps toward the snake enclosures. I take a deep breath and command my feet to follow. The twins rush past me. And then I do it—I just start running toward the enclosures. Where the snakes *lie in wait*.

I tune out my brain and keep running. I'm my own superhero, right?

Rae gets to the gate ahead of me and reaches over to unlatch the door. "It's locked," she says, wiggling it.

And at the sound of those words, the superhero slips away and is replaced by a cold blast of common sense. *Turn back!*

"Maybe we can find a key!" Beatrice says.

"I'll go look for it inside!" I say.

But Rae says, "We don't need one. We can just climb over. Ready?"

I'm not the only the one who hesitates. "What about splinters?" Henry asks.

"What about them?" Rae says.

Henry glances over at me. Last summer, he got a particularly painful splinter in his thumb from a Popsicle stick, and I can see clearly that he doesn't want to deal with another bout of tweezer trauma.

"I thought I saw a few keys in the kitchen drawer." Although I feel cowardly, I'm relieved to have the excuse. "Be right back."

I start heading back to the house. My nerves are on high alert. The sun is especially searing; the air feels particularly hot. I stop for a deep breath in the shade under a wide tree.

Maybe I just need a take two.

Suddenly, something falls from a branch above me—SNAKE, OF COURSE! WHAT WAS I THINKING? I PRACTICALLY ASKED FOR THAT—and I suck in my breath hard and freeze, and hear, "Sorry, my bad!"

I realize that a sneaker, not a snake THANK GOD, has landed on the ground in front of me. Its tongue gapes out. I look up.

Two bare, bronzed legs are dangling from a branch above, one foot exposed. And then a boy emerges, like fruit dropping off a tree. He lands on the ground on one foot and picks up the fallen shoe.

I stare at him, my pulse pounding in my ears. He stares back with eyes that are somewhere on the color spectrum between blue and green. Turquoise? His hair is wild—growing outward like a mane, and brown with gold streaks, like something forgotten in the sun. He wears long swimming trunks as shorts, and his pale-red T-shirt is stained with a blot of purple juice. He looks like something feral—like an undomesticated tree-dwelling species.

I wait for some explanation, but he just stares at me wordlessly.

Then he finally speaks. "I'm Mitchell. I live over there." He points to a small house in the distance, past a low stone wall. It's a tiny cottage, like an old butler's quarters or something.

"I'm Edith," I say. "I mean *Edie*."

He's quiet. His eyes move back in the direction of the snake enclosures.

"Um, so did you know my grandmother, or—"

"Yeah, I did. We were friends," he says. "Who are they?"

"Oh. The tall one's my cousin, Rae and the other two are my brother and sister."

Rae's voice interrupts us. "Hey, Edie! We're in. Forget the key and come back here."

I turn to look. She's inside the gate with Beatrice. Somehow she's convinced Henry to climb over the gate as well.

"Oooh, okay," I say, trying to stay cool. But it's Mitchell who seems to tense up.

"Who's *that*?" Rae calls out.

"A neighbor!" I call back.

"Oh," Rae says. Then she stands a little taller and her voice booms out. *"No bars shall confine me; no walls shall pen me in!"*

"What's she doing?"

"I am free! And my destiny awaits!"

"Oh," I say. "Theatrical lines, I think. I'm not sure if it's Shakespeare—"

"No, I mean . . ." His voice gets tight and panicky. "What is she *doing*?"

"Oh, *oh*. They're just releasing the snakes to take some pictures," I tell him. My words are pretty calm, considering all the inner alarms that are going off.

"Hey, look, you guys—I got one! Henry, make sure you're getting this!" Rae beams. She's holding a gray-and-black spotted snake across her hands. The twins are practically chirping like baby birds with excitement.

Mitchell breathes in sharply. He walks to the enclosure. I follow a distance behind. Then he quickly climb-jumps over the fence.

"Her name's Imelda, and I need you to give her to me right now." He holds out his hands.

"Why?" Rae asks.

"Safety reasons."

"Safety reasons?"

"Just hand her over," Mitchell says.

Rae sighs and surrenders the snake. "Was she going to bite me or something?"

"No, for *her* safety. They get stressed out. It's not good for them." He puts the snake back into its home and gently picks up the other snake that Rae has freed.

"Wait," Rae says. "It's Edie's turn!"

"Yeah!" I say, making my voice strong. Although I'm practically weak with relief that our snake-handling scheme has been shut down, I'm also disappointed that I won't be able to call Taylor tonight and tell her how brave and exciting I've suddenly become.

"These snakes are animals. They're not toys," Mitchell says.

"What are you, some sort of snake patrol?" Rae asks with exasperation.

"Sort of. I help—helped—Petunia take care of them." Mitchell's gaze goes low, as if he's addressing an ant in the grass. "Guess I still do. She loved them. They were her family."

There's a weird silence, and then Henry says, "Not technically. Snakes aren't even mammals!"

"Yeah," Rae says. "*We're* technically her family. So these snakes are *ours* now."

"We have pets!" Beatrice inflates with excitement.

"Yeah, so . . . ," Rae continues, "we can take them out of their cages and play with them, or catch them and set them free, or whatever we want."

I try not to visibly flinch with every word that comes out of Rae's mouth.

Mitchell studies her. "Okay, yeah, I guess you're right. So I should probably tell you how to take care of them."

"Fine. Go ahead," Rae says.

"Okay, you got to feed them once a week."

"Easy enough."

"They like mice," Mitchell says.

"Mice?" Her nose flares.

"Or other small rodents."

"Seriously?" Rae asks. "There's not, like, snake food in a can or something?"

"In a *can*? No, but . . . they only eat about once a week."

Rae's lips are starting to curl.

Mitchell continues. "It's the water that'll keep you really busy. You have to change it a few times a week. They get into it and it gets dirty. And the cage—you got to wipe down the surfaces and change out the—"

"Okay. Never mind," Rae says. "They're all yours, Mitchell. Unless Edie wants to—"

"NO! I mean, I think we're going to be way, *waaay* too busy this summer."

A small smile shows on Mitchell's face. "No worries then. I'll handle it."

"But *I* wanted to catch a snake," Beatrice says.

"Me too," Henry says.

"So." Mitchell looks around. "If you want to catch something, I could, um, teach you how to catch frogs?"

"Frogs!" Beatrice and Henry are as excited as most kids would be for ice cream.

And a gigantic tsunami of relief washes over me. "Frogs! Yes, frogs! Frogs are good! I love frogs!"

Rae looks at me sideways, her forehead crinkling. "*Oh-kay* then?"

"I mean, I always wanted to learn. . . ." I let my voice trail off.

Mitchell turns and leads us down toward Corkscrew Swamp, and I remind myself that it's a long summer ahead—a couple of housefly life spans, probably. So I have plenty of time to start becoming fearless.

"Frogs can't turn their heads, so if you're quiet, you can sneak up from behind," Mitchell explains as we follow him down to Corkscrew Swamp.

"Hey, Mitchell," Beatrice says. "Did you know that a frog sheds its skin once a week—and then eats it?"

"*Everybody* knows that," Henry says.

"That's pretty *ew*," Rae adds.

Beatrice looks at Rae like Rae's the weird one.

"Here's another fact," Beatrice continues. "There's this type of frog called Darwin's frog, and when its tadpoles are born—"

Henry scoffs. "Tadpoles aren't *born*, Beatrice, they're *hatched*!"

"Stop interrupting me! So when the tadpoles are hatched, their dad—"

"It doesn't have to be their *dad*!"

"*Okay*, Henry!" Beatrice seethes. "Anyway, when they're hatched, *a male frog* swallows them. He doesn't eat them, but

56

he *swallows* them into his vocal sac, and they live there for *sixty days*! And after that, he coughs them up, and they're all fully formed frog babies!"

"Beatrice, Henry, you can stop grossing everyone out now," I say, before they delve deeper into amphibian mating habits. *"Please?"*

"That's nothing," Henry starts. "The female Suriname toad—"

"Hey, you all?" Mitchell says in a hushed voice. "If you want to catch frogs, we have to be really quiet."

The twins whisper their okays, thankfully, and we all crouch down near the edge of the swamp. As we settle in, there's a ripple in the water that causes an old half-docked rowboat nearby to groan and sway. I try not to let myself wonder what's causing the ripple.

"Whose boat is that?" Henry whispers.

"No one's," Mitchell whispers back.

"How can it be no one's?"

"It's just been here forever," Mitchell answers quietly. "It belongs here. It's always been here."

"But—"

I shush Henry, but after another few minutes, he asks Mitchell, "Have you ever seen a real alligator?"

Mitchell nods. "Yep."

Oh, no. Do I have bigger things to worry about? Bigger than snakes? "Uh, so . . ." I try to add a carefree quality to my voice, but it just makes me sound squeaky. "Are there . . . *alligators* in this swamp?"

Mitchell looks at me, squinting against the sun, his voice low. "Not really. Used to be, a long time ago, but the fishers killed them off. Then the swamp changed. It got too salty for them. But if you *do* see a gator? Dead or alive?"

How about we don't?

"Just let me know, okay?"

"So, wait, if the swamp's too salty, should we really expect to see an alligator—dead or alive?" Rae asks.

"Yeah, probably not," Mitchell says.

Rae looks at me and mouths, "Oh-*kay*." I smile that secret way back.

Mitchell puts his finger to his lips to quiet us completely. We hear a croak. A frog has jumped and landed on a fallen tree branch a few feet to our left, its back to us. Mitchell slowly knee-crawls up behind it. The frog's croaking stops, maybe as it senses the small mob of us close by. Mitchell inches his arms forward, stealthily. Then, with one quick movement, he closes his hands around the back of the frog and, after a moment, gently lifts a hand away. The small creature sits in the cup of his hand, still and silent.

"He likes you!" Beatrice whispers.

"No," Mitchell whispers back. "He's just stunned."

But the frog suddenly croaks and leaps, plunging into the water with a splash.

"Let me try." Henry hands the camera to Beatrice so she can film him.

Mitchell points them to a log poking out of the edge of the water a short distance away. "You see where that frog's at?" he asks.

"You mean, where that frog *is*," Beatrice corrects him.

"Beatrice!" I whisper-scold. I know that she doesn't mean to be annoying, but that doesn't mean she isn't.

"Maybe they don't go to school here," Henry muses to Beatrice.

I give Rae a look of alarm. She stands up. "Come on, you digotics. Let's go catch some frogs."

"Dizygotes," Henry corrects her.

The three of them head toward the log, Henry way too fast and clumsily. I hear frogs bailing—little splashes of water as they jump from the log into the swamp.

"Sorry about that," I say to Mitchell. "They didn't mean—"

He shakes his head. "It's no big deal."

I wish for something clever to say. It would just be nice to have a laugh with him—if only to make up for the twins' comments. A fly buzzes around us. Mitchell runs a hand through his wild hair. I notice that even though he's a little shaggy looking, he's not *bad* looking. He's *interesting* looking.

I've heard people say that about me before. For this first time, I see how it can be a compliment.

We hear a croak nearby. Mitchell turns toward me, his eyebrows raised. He nods toward the edge of the swamp, where I can see a fat green frog growing even fatter with every breath.

"Your turn," Mitchell says.

Even though my nerves start to chatter among themselves, I slowly push myself to a crouch, and I notice that the twins and Rae are also quietly watching me. *Not a snake*, I tell myself. *Not. A. Snake.*

I lunge for it. But the frog is too fast for me. It leaps off, plunging into the water, and I land on my belly in the mud. I peel myself up, feeling ridiculous, noticing the ugly brown stains on the front of my T-shirt and shorts. But instead of sounding amused, my laugh comes out like a statement. "Ha ha ha."

"Good try," Mitchell says when I sit back down. "Just next time, try not to be so scared."

"Scared?" Is it really that obvious? I feel as ashamed as I would if he'd told me my underwear tag was showing.

"If you're calm, they're calm," he explains. Then he points to a tree stump. On it, a smaller frog sits waiting. Then he looks back up at me and gives me a go-for-it nod.

I try to think *calm*. I try to breathe *calm*. I try to look *calm*. And then I crawl up behind the frog, like I'm in slow motion. When I'm close enough, I sweep forward, gently cupping my hands around the tiny creature. Even though my skin is prickling with creeped-out goose bumps, I feel myself smiling.

The frog squirms in my hands—UGH—and I open my palms to release it. It springs away. "Did you see that?" I ask Mitchell.

Before he can answer, we hear a shriek. A frog leaps from Henry's hand. He is holding his hands as far away from his body as possible, his eyebrows squeezing together tightly, his mouth open with alarm. "It did something!"

"Oh." Mitchell grimaces. "It probably just peed on you. Sometimes they do that."

"I guess they don't teach that in school," I say to Mitchell, and he looks at me, a dimple forming in his cheek. My face feels a little warm.

"Edith!" It's my mom's voice calling out. Her worry is making its way all the way down to the swamp's edge. She's obviously discovered us all missing in action.

"*Carp!*" I say. "We better go back."

"*Carp?*" Rae asks. "Isn't that some type of fish?"

Believe it or not, sometimes I forget what a Whitman's Sampler box of freaks my family is. It's only possible for five minutes max. "My parents—well, we're not allowed to say *crap.* So that's what we say instead." I nervously clear my throat.

"So you speak in typo?" Rae jokes.

"Edith!" Her voice is getting nearer.

"Let's get back," I say. "It sounds like she's starting to freak out."

And then we hear, "Hey, sport!" It's Uncle A.J.

"Great. So is he," Rae says.

That's *freaking out*?

I'm about to say good-bye to Mitchell when I turn and see my mom. "Oh, *honey*," she says, noticing the mud on my shirt. "What happened?"

"We were catching frogs and you're supposed to sneak up behind them and Edith slipped in the mud and the frog got away!" Beatrice says.

"Aunt Hannah, this is Mitchell. He's a neighbor," Rae says.

"Oh, hello, Mitchell. I'm Hannah Posey-Preston. Petunia's daughter. Pardon me. I was just a little worried about the kids." She smiles and extends her hand in the same professional-convention way, and he shakes it.

"We wanted to catch snakes, Mom!" Henry says.

"Yeah, but he made us put the snakes back!" Beatrice says.

Mitchell says, "Sorry, I had to. Petunia taught me how to

take care of them, and they don't like being taken out of their enclosures like that."

"I have to agree with Mitchell, kids. You really shouldn't disrupt the snakes."

"Well, it's not like they're poisonous," Rae says.

"No, but you *can* catch salmonella from snakes. Anyway, it's best not to disrupt their environment. They *are* living creatures."

"Mitchell already said that," Beatrice says.

My mom smiles at him. "Mitchell, we'll have to have you over for dinner sometime. We'd like to thank you properly for taking good care of Petunia's snakes."

Really, Mom?

"Oh, uh . . . sure," he says, but he looks uncomfortable.

"Great! Okay, come on, kids. Go get cleaned up."

My mom and the twins start up the path.

I turn to Mitchell. "Thanks for the frog lessons."

"Yeah, sure," Mitchell says. "Catch you all later."

And this time our eyes connect, something strange happens. It's like there's an extra second added to the day. But Rae grabs my hand and pulls me out of my mini time warp, and we say bye to Mitchell and start back toward the house.

"So, what do you think of Snake Boy?" Rae asks me.

"Oh." I let out a gust of breath, suddenly aware that I've been holding it. "He's kind of—crazy," I say. It's the one thing that I've found I can say when I don't know *what* to say, because crazy can be either good or bad.

"I know, right? Nice enough, I guess, but kind of a weirdo," she says.

"Sorry about the snakes," I say. And in a way, I mean it. I wish I naturally had the guts to catch a snake bare-handed, like Rae does, and didn't have to work so hard to pretend that I do.

She pulls out her phone and looks at it. "Well, I'm not! Look at this, Edie, already eighty-two likes!"

I wonder what it's like to have eighty-two likes—let alone eighty-two friends. I think again about Taylor. I'd be happy to have just that one.

Chapter 7

Scoop

"**I**'m king of the world!"

I'm crouched in the rear basket of what turns out to be not a bike, but an adult tricycle—my grandmother's preferred mode of transportation. I'm holding on to the back of Rae's seat for dear life while she stands up on the pedals, shouting out lines from some of her favorite movies. In the four days we've been here, I've learned she does this a lot.

"You ever see that one, Edie? *Titanic*?"

"No," I say. I realize I look like an idiot, but as it turns out, the shame of being stuffed into a trike basket is only slightly outranked by the danger of first-degree burns. Metal is a way-too-effective conductor for the ninety-plus degrees of sticky Florida heat, and in my shorts and T-shirt, I have way too many vulnerable spots.

"You should. It's a classic!"

With the adults distracted by decaying roof beams at the house, Rae and I are on a covert mission into town to find a metal detector. We're looking for a hardware store. While I still haven't caught a snake, Rae's eager to start a new adventure—item two on the list, "discover hidden treasures"—especially if it results in a post-worthy bling shot. Hopefully our parents won't even notice we're gone.

We sail by a few old houses and a small church. "Are you sure you know where we're going?" I ask.

"Don't worry. This town's the size of a Tater Tot."

We ride by a large abandoned building with a painted-over sign stretching its span, just a few letters slightly visible under the coat of thick white paint. It looks like it used to be something significant—a theater, maybe, or an auditorium. Whatever it was, it seems to have outlived its purpose and now stands empty, forgotten. Even though everything around me feels scalding hot—the air, the sun, the trike's basket—I get a little chill as we ride past.

Rae, on the other hand, is too busy carpe dieming to notice. She pushes the pedals hard and stands up to soar. Releasing one hand into air, she calls out, "I'm flying, Jack! I'm flying!" It must be another quote from *Titanic*.

Just then, a bike bolts across the road in front of us, and Rae jams on the brakes. The trike makes a screech and my body jolts forward. I manage not to topple over by grabbing onto the side of the basket. My scream sounds more like a wail.

"Hey!" Rae yells to the fleeing wild-haired kid. *"Watch it!"*

He disappears around the corner.

"He kind of looked like Mitchell," I say as I catch my breath.

"Snake Boy?" Rae asks.

"Yeah. Him."

But then two boys charge across our path on foot. They're laughing, running after him. "Hey, come back, Ed!"

"Well, guess it's *not* him," Rae says. "Apparently this town is full of Snake Boy look-alikes."

"Weird," I say. And then I notice that we're just across the street from a hardware store. AUGUSTUS TOOLS, the sign says in capital letters. Underneath, in a slanted font, it reads *AND TREATS*. Through the big front window, you can see a small ice-cream counter.

"Ice cream!" Rae's face lights up. "Finally! Something in this town that I like."

We leave the trike on the sidewalk and go in. A bell jingles when we open the door, and a man in a red apron looks at us in a not-so-welcoming way. There's a sign behind the counter that says NO UNACCOMPANIED MINORS. I'm pretty sure that applies to us, and I feel a little self-conscious, like I'm a member of some unwanted population.

Rae notices my hesitation. "Come on. We have as much right to be here as anyone else. We're paying customers," she says, and charges on.

"Help you?" the man in the apron asks.

It's a small store. Besides the ice-cream counter, there are only four rows of shelves, all jam-packed. In addition to tools, Augustus seems to carry a random supply of household items. Cake mixers, turkey basters, food coloring, egg slicers, and very odd things like a bone-shaped plastic apparatus designed to better scrape condiments out of their jars: the Mayoknife. There's no sign of any metal detectors.

"First things first," Rae says, and takes a seat at the ice-cream counter, as if she's an eagerly anticipated guest. She offers her smile like a gift. "We'd like some ice cream."

"Your parents around?" the man asks.

"They're not, but . . ." She puts a twenty-dollar bill on the counter. "I hope that's okay."

The man glances at the money. I settle onto the stool next to Rae.

There's an old woman sitting on a stool at the counter farther down. One pair of glasses hangs on a chain around her neck; she has another pair perched on her head. She wears bright-orange lipstick, and her dyed hair nearly matches the color. She's watching a tiny TV that's propped up on a shelf—a soap opera without the sound.

"We hear you've got the best ice cream in Pinne," Rae says.

His eyebrows shoot up. *"Pinn-ey?"*

"Isn't that how it's said?" she asks. I have the same question.

"It's Pa-*inny*," he says to Rae. "Try again."

"Pi-*inny*?" Rae aks.

"I didn't say *Pinny*. You make it sound like a one-cent coin! No, listen: Pa-*inny*," he says again. "There's sorta like a pause in there."

"Pa-*hinny*."

He smirks. "Not Pa-*hinny*. Where you getting the H sound? See, look." He takes a letter from his mail stack and runs his finger over the town's name. "P-I-N-N-E. No H."

"No A either," Rae says.

He shakes his head. "Never mind. What can I get you?"

Rae just sighs happily and glances at the list of flavors written in chalk above the cash register. There are only three—vanilla, chocolate, and something called Surprise Me! "What do you think, cuz?"

"Ya'll are cousins?" the man asks, looking from me to her, no doubt seeing the vast differences between us.

"Yep," Rae says.

"Welles, give those squirrels a glass of water," says the old lady.

I look for squirrels. Stuffed squirrels, in particular. Maybe mounted on a wall, like Herbie, or on a wooden stand, like Albert/Odysseus. It seems like stuffing and mounting is the thing to do in this area. But there are none.

The man's expression goes a little soft. "I'm sorry about that. She's a little . . ." He does a finger-loopy gesture next to his head. Then he fills two tall glasses with water and passes them across the counter to us. "It comes and goes. She's got the auld-timer's, but she's still my ma."

"Always liked the squirrel. Smart thing, a squirrel."

"Ma, these are *girls*, they're *not*—" he starts, but interrupts himself. "Keep having to remind myself that the doctor said no use arguing."

"It's just the droppings that I can't stand—"

"*Ma!*" Welles looks down and shakes his head.

"Well, she's got a point," Rae says.

The man smiles. Then he extends his hand, first to Rae, then to me. "Welles Augustus," he says.

"I'm Rae."

"And I'm Edie." Saying the name is like trying on a new pair of jeans that I desperately want to fit.

"Pleased to meet you. All right, squirrels." He gestures toward the chalkboard. "Three flavors. What can I get you?"

"What's a Surprise Me?" I ask him.

He does a quick look back at his mother to make sure she's not paying attention. She seems to be entranced by the silent drama on the small television. He puts a hand along one side of his face, like he's telling us a secret. "I don't actually know. That's what my ma gets up to with her ice-cream maker. Keeps her occupied, you know." He winks.

I give him a smile and choose vanilla. Rae chooses Surprise Me. The seize-the-day kind of choice. Of course. I feel a little ashamed of my vanilla.

"So where y'all from?"

"I'm from L.A.," Rae says. Even where she's from sounds cool.

"Well, Cally-fornia," he says. "You a— Hey! Haven't I seen you on the TV?"

She winces. "A couple stupid commercials."

"Commercials! Get a load of that! For . . . uh, remind me?" Welles steps back. "Wait, I know. You were bouncing around with a chicken!"

"Pollo Mio," she mumbles.

"That's right! Well, I'll be," he says, with a huge grin on his face.

I study her for a second, feeling the difference between us. I can't help but wonder how it feels to stand out—in some sort of celebrated way, not in the sore-thumb way I sometimes do. Even if Rae's dismissive of her national TV spot, this Welles person is clearly impressed.

"And what about you?" Welles turns to me. "You from L.A. too?"

I sigh. "No," I say, "Boston." And prepare for the response we usually get whenever we travel and are asked the same question.

"Ah, *Baaas*-tin." *There it is.* "So what brings you to Pinne?" he asks. Those three syllables, that hanging pause.

"Our parents grew up here," I say.

"Maybe I know them. What are their names?"

"You probably remember my dad, A.J. Posey," Rae says.

"Oh, well, let's see. An A.J.?" He seems to think about it. Then he says, "Oh! *A.J.* You mean Hannah's brother!" He looks at me. "You Hannah's daughter, then?"

I nod. Oddly, he seems way more interested in my nerdy mom than my friendly uncle.

"Now, *holy*. Hannah *Posey*?" He slaps the counters and breaks into a full-faced grin. "I've been wondering where she went off to. She in town?" he asks, but immediately shakes his head, looking down at the counter. "Course she'd be. On account of her mother passing. That right?"

I nod.

"Well, my condolences. She sure was *something*." He turns to the old lady. "Hey, *Ma*. This is Hannah's daughter."

His ma swats at a fly.

He tries again. "Ma, remember Petunia? These are Petunia's grands."

"Petunia's?" She scrunches up her face.

"That's right."

"I never liked her."

"Ma!" he scolds, and looks over at us with an apologetic half smile.

"So you knew her?" Even though I shouldn't be surprised, with Pinne being so tiny, it still feels a little strange that everyone knew her except for me.

He smiles. "Sure did. Smart as a whip. Stubborn as a mule. And wild as a thicket of blackberries."

There's a look of unmistakable admiration on his face, and I feel a little puff of pride about the grandmother I only wish I had met.

"You know," he says, his eyes really coming to life. "I remember one time, she used to pick me up before school sometimes, and one day she was like, 'Welles, I have a car, and we have the whole day ahead—'"

Wait. *Before school?*

"Hang on," I interrupt him. "Petunia picked you up for *school*?"

"Petunia? No, I thought you were asking about your mom. Hannah."

I blink, confused. I guess he has Hannah on the brain.

"Well, go ahead, what happened?" Rae asks, smiling in a mischievous way.

"Aw, well, uh, you know, I'm having trouble remembering now." He tilts his head, a hand wrapping around the back of his neck. Then he seems to get a brilliant idea. "Hey, you girls want any more ice cream?"

"No, thanks, I'm full," Rae says. I've eaten all of mine, but Rae's barely taken a spoonful of hers. She says in a quiet voice that only I can hear, "Tastes like hooves."

"WHAT IN THE SAM HILL?" Welles's ma is up from her stool, her arms flailing about.

"What's the matter, Ma?"

"We've been burgled! Must have been a cat burglar! Snuck in here while I was making the ice cream!"

"What's missing?"

"My spare pair!"

"Ma?"

"Damn thief took my spare pair of glasses!"

"Ma!"

74

"Call the nine one one, Welles! Call Elwayne!"

"Ma, lift your hand—"

"Fine, I'll do it myself!"

"They're on your head, Ma!"

"My what?"

"Your head."

Her hand flies to her pink-red fluff of hair. "Oh," she says.

Welles chuckles. "All right, looks like Ma's needing her break. I'm going to close up shop and drive her home soon. Wasn't there something else that you needed?" He walks over to the shelves. "How 'bout a Chick-a-Dee egg separator?"

"Actually—" Rae tries.

"Or a finger fork?" He slides a contraption over his finger. The end of it has four prongs.

"Actually, we were looking for a metal detector," Rae tells him.

"*A metal detector!*" Welles's eyes get big.

"You have one?" Rae asks.

"Oh, boy, *do I*! Y'all wait here."

When Welles reappears, he's brandishing a long instrument—a generously padded handle on one end, a large, round sensor on the other. "Edie, Rae, may I introduce you to my dear friend, the Bounty Hunter. Professional, four-mode operation, a ground-balance monitor, a blanker system—"

I think he's in love with this device. He's practically in a trance, talking about a "sniff mode" and a "notching system."

"Great, we'll take it," Rae says.

He beams. "Okay, girls, that'll be a hundred and sixty-two dollars."

"Oh." I realize that the only way we can afford it is if we buy it on credit and repay it with all this buried treasure we may or may not find. Welles is apologetic but doesn't take us up on our offer.

On the bright side, he sends us off with a toothpick truck—a tiny truck-shaped toothpick dispenser. It's not exactly a hidden treasure, but when Rae smiles like we're sharing some sort of secret, it feels like a decent consolation prize.

The ride downtown might have had us practically flying, but the ride home is a different story altogether. While "flying," Rae accidentally veers us right over a nail in the road. The front tire becomes a little droopy, then saggy, and then, halfway home, it flattens into the hot black asphalt. We end up having to push the trike home on foot.

When we've finally made it home and we're wheeling it back toward the garage, I notice Mitchell. He's walking down the path between our houses with a bucket in one hand—probably some roadkill he's about to give to the snakes, I shudder to think. With his loose T-shirt and the way the sunlight shoots through his manelike hair, I realize he's the boy we almost collided with earlier.

"Hey, that *was* him," I tell Rae. "He was going fast, but that was him."

He overhears me. His eyes snap to mine.

"Wait, that was *you*?" Rae asks. "Don't those guys know your name?"

He shrugs.

I ask, "Who were they?"

"The Pinne Mafia." He smiles, and that dimple pops into his cheek again.

"The Mafia, huh?" Rae says, grinning back. "Well, you almost ran right into us."

"I thought you were going to kill me with that thing." He gestures toward the trike.

"If I wanted to kill you, you'd be dead already," she says in this mysteriously low voice.

Mitchell looks surprised. "*The Godfather*! You've *seen* it?"

"Of course," Rae says. "It's a cinematic masterpiece. Who hasn't?"

Me. That would be me. I've heard of it, just enough to know that I wouldn't be allowed to watch it, not in a million years.

"Leave the gun, take the cannoli," Mitchell says in a gravelly voice, and the two of them break into a fit of laughter. I smile awkwardly, adjust my glasses, and wish I wasn't stuck on the outskirts of their little private joke.

"Well, you don't have to worry about us killing you again—this thing is out of commission. We ran over a nail." Rae makes a *womp-womp* sound and says, "Anyway, where were you going so fast?"

"I was hoping to find an alligator," he says.

"Oh, yeah. Dead or alive, right?" Rae jokes. "Well, did you?"

He frowns. "Nope."

Forget the dimple. I remind myself that he's a reptile lover, probably even a certified, card-carrying one—and what's a dimple anyway? A dent in someone's cheek? Big deal!

And then I hear, "Mom! She's *heeere!*"

Beatrice stares at us from the porch.

"Great," I seethe, although I'm glad for the quick exit from this conversation. "My mom's going to have a fit."

"Let me handle it," Rae says. She waves over her shoulder at Mitchell, and we make our way up to the house and into the kitchen, just as my mom charges into it.

"Hi, Aunt Hannah!" Rae smiles.

"Girls! Where were you? I looked everywhere!"

"Aunt Hannah, we just met an old classmate of yours! His name is Welles Augustus, and he runs a hardware shop that serves ice cream—can you believe it? He says you should come say hi." Then she lowers her voice and puts her hand to the side of her mouth. "Just stay away from the Surprise Me."

My mom puts a polite smile on her face. "Well, that's very nice. But Edith . . ." She turns to me. "Do I understand this right? You girls went downtown? On your *own*?"

Rae seems oblivious. "Yeah. Luckily Petunia had that trike."

"Hold on," my mom says, all traces of her smile completely gone. Her hand goes over her heart. "Do you mean to tell me that you rode Petunia's *tricycle* into town?"

"Mom, *please*." I beg her with my eyes to try to let this go. "We're fine, okay? It's fine."

"Edith, no, it is *not* fine! You've could've had an accident!"

Uncle A.J. comes into the kitchen. "Oh, come on, Hannah. I think they can handle themselves okay."

"A.J., they're still children, I might remind you!"

Children.

"Do you know how many bicyclists are injured in motor-vehicle collisions? More than forty thousand a year!"

"Hannah, if you want to talk about research, I can guarantee you that most research tells you that exercise is actually good for kids."

My mom opens her mouth, but before she can say anything else, Rae clasps her hands to her own heart and says, "Aunt Hannah, I'm so, so sorry if we worried you. It was my idea, not Edie's. We should have told someone—I mean, *asked* someone."

The should language. Rae's speaking it. My mom sighs and releases her shoulders away from her ears, and sends us off to the study. Maybe I should be relieved that we haven't been punished, but I'm not. I know she'll be keeping a closer eye on me. How am I going to do all the things on Petunia's list if my mother won't let me out of her sight?

In the study, Rae sits at the desk and tries to check her phone. "Welcome to the inter*not*."

"No service?" I ask.

"It must be down. *Great*." She puts her phone on the desk and looks at me. "You okay?"

"Yeah, I'm fine," I say, although I'm still annoyed with my mother.

"Okay? If you say so." She jumps up from the desk chair and runs over to a rolling ladder in front of the bookshelves. She climbs up a few rungs. "Hey, Edie, give me a push."

I give the ladder a little push. It only edges over an inch.

"Oh, come on, Edie. A *real* push."

So I push harder, and she laughs and swings out a little to give it a little more speed. Then it stops, and she looks at me.

"Edie, seriously, what's wrong?"

I shrug. "It's just my mother."

"What about her?"

"You saw how she is. She treats me like I'm four sometimes!"

She leans back from the ladder, looking at me upside
down. "She's just, you know, one of those worry kinds of
moms. Now, this time, push like you mean it."

I give her the biggest, strongest push I can, and she yells,
"Wheeeeeeee!" and I miss Taylor more than ever. At least she
knows what it's like dealing with a hovering mother.

It was actually our overprotective moms that brought
Taylor and me together in the first place: a big overnight
class trip to New York City in the fourth grade. My mom
wouldn't let me go because of the sleeping arrangements:
with four girls to a hotel room, she was sure we'd suffer sleep
deprivation. Taylor's mom wouldn't let her go because of her
allergies—there was a chance Taylor would accidentally eat
something that would make her sick. So when the class went
away, our parents let us hang out together all day, enjoying
old Harry Potter movies and stuffing ourselves with dairy-
and gluten-free treats. The rest is history.

Or it was. Until Sophi Angelo entered the picture.

A *ding* comes from Rae's phone on the desk. "Service,
finally!" she says, and jumps off the ladder.

As she checks her phone, I sneak upstairs. I *have* to call
Taylor. Even if there's not much to brag about yet. I just need

to hear her voice. On the landing at the top of the stairs, I pick up an old-fashioned phone, yellow, almost gold, with a curly cord. I'm glad I have my mom's gift for memorization, and I punch in the ten digits.

"Hello?"

"Hi, Mrs. McGowan. It's Edie. Is Taylor there?"

"Sorry, who is it?"

"Oh, it's—it's Edith."

"Oh, Edith! How are you? How's Florida?"

"It's okay, it's—"

"Hot as heck, I bet."

"Yes, it is. So . . . uh, is Taylor home?"

"Oh, no. I guess she didn't tell you?"

"No . . . uh, *tell me?*"

"Oh, I'm sorry—I'm sure she meant to before she left. But honey, she's at Camp Berrybrook."

I recognize the name. My throat tightens and my stomach sinks. Camp Berrybrook. Sophi's beloved summer camp. Where they will have adventures—excitement galore, no doubt—without me.

"You let her go?"

"Well, she'd been wanting to, and a slot opened, so . . ."

"But what about the gluten?"

Her mom pauses, then says, "Well, honey, the camp director knows all about her allergies, of course—"

"And dairy? What if they serve ice cream?"

"Edith, you're a good friend to be so concerned, but Taylor's really become good at managing her allergies on her own lately, and she's ready to do some new things, so . . ."

New nonboring things. With new nonboring friends.

"So, I'll see her on visiting day, and I'll make sure she calls you—"

"When's that?"

"Oh, visiting day?" she asks. "It's in a few weeks."

"Can you be more specific?"

She gives me the date—it's three weeks away. I give her the address and phone number for Petunia's house, and she gives me Taylor's address at Camp Berrybrook in case I want to write a letter. But when we hang up, I just stare at it through the tears that are filling my eyes. I mean, what would I even write to Taylor? That I *didn't* catch a snake? That my mom still treats me like I'm a toddler, while hers seems to suddenly think she's an adult? That I'm as boring as I was two weeks ago, when I last saw her?

"Hey," I hear. I turn and see Rae at the foot of the stairs, looking up at me.

"Hey!" *Carp!* I blink, and a tear spills out. Luckily she doesn't seem to notice. I quickly wipe it away.

"You sneaking off to make a call means one thing."

"It does?"

"Mm-hmm." She smiles. "Klaus."

"Oh. I, uh—" Here's my chance to right this wrong. Maybe I can just ditch this imaginary boyfriend and be done with this charade. *Carefully*, of course. I don't want her to know that I'm such a loser I had to make him up. "Um, you know what? I'm not even sure we're still going out."

"Couldn't get ahold of him, huh?" She sighs. "I know. I hate when that happens. I mean, with Leo back home in California, and me *here*, it's like, how are we going to keep this together?"

"Yeah." A gentle snort seeps out. *Ugh.*

"But I have another question for you."

I brace myself.

"Why on earth don't you have a phone? I've had one since I was eight!"

It feels almost shameful that my parents won't let me have one, but at least it gives me a reason for not having frequent long, lingering, possibly lovelorn conversations and texting sessions with Klaus all summer.

"I'll probably get one when we get back," I say. And that part's true. The part I don't tell her is that my parents have talked about getting me a Jitterbug phone. It's made for old people. No internet, no texting, just phone service. With a dial tone, to avoid further confusing the elderly and demented.

"Yeah, you definitely need one," Rae says.

"Very true," I say. And it *is*. I mean, I know a girl who's Amish, and even *she* has one. My parents, however, don't find that a compelling argument.

"Well, you can use mine whenever you want," she says.

"Thanks," I say.

"Sure." She gives me a big smile, like that solves all my problems. I only wish that it did.

Chapter 8

This Old House

Rae and I are in the kitchen, eating Pop-Tarts and drinking coffee. Black with sugar.

Apparently she's been drinking coffee since she was ten, and making it for my uncle since she was eight. When we came down to the kitchen this morning and saw the new coffee machine that our parents splurged on, Rae didn't ask me if I wanted a cup of coffee. She asked how I *took* it. But while I was thinking about how to answer that question, she said (thankfully), "Let's hope you don't take milk, because this milk smells a little weird."

So I guess I don't take milk. I take a small sip. It's wretched.

I try not to let it show on my face.

But Rae's not looking at me—she's checking her phone. "Sorry to disappoint you, cuz, but my weather app says clear skies today and tomorrow. Still no hurricanes to dance in. I say we stick with item two and keep up the treasure hunt. At least we'll be out of the house."

For the past few days since our ride downtown, my mom's barely let us out of the study. But today we're supposed to be clearing out the garage, and I'm thrilled. Maybe we can sneak off and pursue the list once we're out from under her watchful eye.

My mom walks into the kitchen. "Morning," she says. She walks behind me and gives me a little kiss on the head. Then she notices what I'm drinking. "Oh, *Edith*, coffee?"

I sigh—but it's more relief than frustration—and say, "*Okay*, Mom! I won't drink it!"

The screen door squeaks open, and my dad walks into the kitchen from outside. The twins follow behind him. "Good morning, everyone!" He sounds like Mister Rogers. "Thought we'd grab a bite before we start off on our search for Bachman's warbler."

"You're getting a late start, aren't you, Walt?" my mom asks.

"We got a little waylaid by a, uh, stray cat," my dad says.

"A nonexistent one!" Henry says.

Beatrice juts her chin forward. "A kitten! He's real!"

"Then how come you're the only one who's seen it, Beatrice?" Henry says. "I'm the one wearing the glasses."

"Okay, twins, there's no need to argue. Let's have a little grub, huh?" He smiles. "Get it—*grub*?"

They just stare at him.

"Bird humor," he explains.

"Oh, now I get it, Dad," Beatrice says.

"Well, I *get* it," Henry says. "But that doesn't mean it makes me want to laugh."

"You're a tough audience, Henry," my dad says, reaching into a cabinet with a missing door to get his Tupperware container of gorp, his acronym for "good ol' raisins and peanuts." But he pulls it down with a concerned look on his face. "Well, *scab buckets!*"

Uncle A.J. stomps into the kitchen in his heavy boots. "Let me guess. Mice?" he asks, without much of a reaction.

"Mice?" My dad holds the container out so everyone can see it. The top has been gnawed right through. "Actually, it's hardly *mice* we're looking at." His voice remains stubbornly upbeat. "It's rats."

The kitchen fills with several sounds. There are *oohs* (the twins) and *eews* (Rae) and loud sighs (Mom) and well-hidden panic attacks (me). Cabinet doors creak open and slam shut as Uncle A.J. starts surveying the kitchen for more signs of the rats.

"Great. Oh, just *great*. We've got to get rid of them ASAP," my mom says.

"Get rid of them? I thought we liked animals," Beatrice argues. "I thought we were supposed to be nice to them."

"We do. We *are*," my dad says.

"Then why can't we keep them?"

"Oh!" Henry says. "We could do the Dr. Panksepp experiment!" He's talking about an experiment in which a scientist recorded rats being tickled and laughing.

"No, I mean, we could get a Habitrail and keep them as pets," Beatrice argues.

"Beatrice, honey, we can't keep them," my mother says. "These aren't lab rats. These are *wild* ones. They carry all sorts of diseases."

"Afraid she's right, kiddos," my dad says, and starts listing diseases. "Leptovirus, hantavirus—"

"Oh, yeah, *Hannah* virus." Uncle A.J.'s laugh booms. "I know that one pretty well."

My mom rolls her eyes, and everyone laughs except for Henry, who looks a little puzzled.

"Well, all joking aside, looks like we need to come up with a rat plan," my dad says.

"Yeah—it's called an exterminator," Uncle A.J. says.

"I'm not crazy about the poisons they use," my mom says.

"Wait! How about a natural predator?" Beatrice gets suddenly excited. "We could use my kitten! We could name him Aristotle, and he'd be part of the family. He can sleep in our room!"

"Beatrice, this isn't a petting zoo," my mom says. That's her general approach to the idea of getting a pet. It's a source of tension between her and, oh, everyone else in our family. For, of course, different reasons. Beatrice wants a pet to play with; Henry wants a pet to train; my dad wants a pet to teach with; and *I* simply want some normal company.

"All right, everyone. We've all got work to do," A.J. says, and shoos everyone out of the kitchen.

"Henry, Beatrice, why don't you help Rae and Edith clean out the garage?" my dad says.

"What?" I say. "I thought you were taking them out to find the warbler!"

"I'm afraid I'll be more useful here today," he says.

"Hey, Walt, you don't have to stay," Uncle A.J. says. "It's fine—totally fine, you know—if you want to take the twins out looking for that wobbler."

"Well, we're a team here, aren't we? I think we should drill some holes into these walls so we can peek in and get a good look at exactly how bad this rat problem really is."

Uncle A.J. shoots a somewhat pleading look at my mom. I

wonder if this look has anything to do with my dad's "help-ing out" yesterday and the broken rafter that resulted from his bad hammer swing.

My mom gives my uncle A.J. an apologetic look and says, "Walt, maybe instead of, uh, damaging the walls, we could come up with a solution we can all agree on."

Uncle A.J. surrenders. "Okay, kids. All of you, get crack-ing on the garage."

Rae and I try to argue, but it's useless. If there was any hidden treasure on our horizon, it seems like it's quickly being stolen away.

Out in the garage, Rae takes another look at the trike. With the front tire deflated, it looks like a droopier version of itself. She sighs. "Well, it doesn't look like we'll be going anywhere on this thing again anytime soon."

"Where did you guys go, anyway?" Beatrice asks.

"Just downtown," I tell her.

"Why?"

"What do you mean, why? Why *not*?" Rae says.

"Yeah, why not?" I echo.

Beatrice looks at me, a little puzzled. "You're acting weird, Edith."

"I'm acting normal," I say. "This is what normal people my age do. They go places. And do things."

"What things?" Henry asks.

"Like try to buy metal detectors?" Rae says, breaking into a laugh. I do too.

Henry looks up. "Why did you want to buy a metal detector?"

I look over at Rae. It seems like the list should stay between us. Letting the twins in on it would mean questioning, dissecting, and shredding it into trivia categories. So I say, "We were just curious. You know, if there are any old family treasures, it would be a shame to let them go to some new owner—"

"No, I mean why would you want to buy a metal detector? We can just build our own."

"How?" I ask.

"By making a radio frequency signal."

"Oh," Rae says. "Of course. Why didn't *I* think of that?"

He shrugs. "Probably because you go to an arts school."

"Wasn't a real question," Rae says, giving him a look.

"But you—"

"Henry," I interrupt, "why don't you just show us how?"

He puts down the camera and runs into the house.

"Is he serious?" Rae asks.

"Yeah, I think he is." And for that moment, I feel grateful for his little weird-genius mind.

When he comes back, he's carrying a box. It's full of the

old electronics that he's apparently been scavenging from the closets and nooks of the house since we got here last week. He turns on the radio, and we hear scrambled voices and static. "First, you have to go to the high end of the AM band, but you don't want a real station," he explains. He plays with the dial until he finds steady static. Then he turns it up.

"Does it have to be so loud?" I ask over the nerve-jangling sound.

"Yes," he says. He takes an old calculator out of the box and turns that on. Then he places the radio and the calculator together, back to back, and the radio sound changes into a loud whirring.

I help Henry tape the two devices together with some smiley-face-patterned duct tape—no doubt from the shelves of Augustus Tools and Treats—and Henry looks up. "It's ready."

Rae looks a little dubious, but her expression changes when Henry hovers it close to a box of stray nails and the radio makes a static beeping sound. The closer it gets to the box, the more distinct the beeping.

Rae says. "Can I see it?"

Henry hands the metal detector over to her. She waves it around in front of him. It's just making the usual static. "Well, I guess you *are* human," she declares. Then she starts wandering around the garage, setting off the device's beeping with hubcaps and screws and tools. "This is so cool!"

Henry smiles a little proudly.

"Come on, you guys, maybe the pirates of the Caribbean were here." In a grand, performance-ready voice, she says, "I regret nothing. Ever." And we follow her out the door.

The homemade metal detector whirs its static sound as we slowly make our way past Mitchell's house.

"Hihihihi," we hear. I notice a small face pressing into the screen door.

"Hey there, kid," Rae says.

Mitchell appears in the doorway, behind the small boy. He opens the door. "Oh, hey," he says. "This is Colvin, my brother."

"Hi, Colvin," I say, and wave.

"Hello," Beatrice and Henry say.

"Hihihihi."

The twins stare at him like he's an exotic lab specimen, while Colvin keeps spewing out the greeting.

"How do you get him to stop?" Henry asks Mitchell.

"I wish I knew," Mitchell says. Our eyes flicker to meet and bounce away.

"Halt," Beatrice says to Colvin. It's ineffective.

"He probably needs specific instructions," Henry says, and then he tries. "Please close your mouth."

"No!" Colvin runs past them into the yard.

"Now what's he doing?" Henry calls out.

"Running," Mitchell says.

"Why?" Beatrice asks.

"I think he wants you guys to chase him," Mitchell explains.

"For what purpose?" Henry asks.

"Just do it!" Rae says.

The twins run off behind Colvin, who is surprisingly fast. I watch them chase each other aimlessly around in the yard. They almost look like normal children.

Mitchell sits down on the front steps of his house. He looks over at the strange device Rae holds in her hand and then shoots her a questioning glance.

In a gravelly voice that I recognize from their *Godfather* banter, Rae says, "Don't ask me about my business." And they both laugh.

I want to be part of this. I try to remember the other *Godfather* quote they had flung around the other day. What was it? And then it comes to me. "Leave the gun," I say. "Take the cannellini!"

"Oh, you mean cannoli," Rae says.

Whoops. I redden. And out of embarrassment, I start to laugh. Well, I snort. It just comes out that way, and I try to laugh to cover it up, but it ends up in more snorts, so I pretend I've developed some sort of cough. Rae gives me a couple gentle slaps on the back.

"You okay?" Mitchell asks.

"Yeah, I . . . uh, inhaled a bug, I think." Which actually does happen in these parts of Florida.

"Honestly, Edie, you've *got* to see it. It really is a cinematic masterpiece," Rae says. "It'll change you forever."

But for the moment, I'm less interested in a movie that will change me forever, and more interested in a magical feat that will somehow help me instantly disappear.

The twins seem happily occupied with their chasing game, but Rae and I are ready to press on with our treasure hunt.

"So, Mitchell," Rae says. "If you watch the twins for a few minutes, we'll give you first dibs on any treasure we find with this thing."

"Yeah, good luck with that." He gives her a single-cheek smile. "Go ahead. I've got to be here with Colvin anyway."

Rae and I thank him and tell him we'll be quick. Then we make our way down the road. We have several false alarms: a bottle cap, a stray metal wire, an old spoon. Then we find ourselves in front of another small house, with the detector screeching out a high pitch. There's a car in the driveway, gray and dented, long enough to belong in another era. On the car's bumper is a sticker: I PLAY ACCORDION, in big letters. Underneath, in smaller letters, AND I VOTE.

Rae turns off the device, but our scuttling around has alerted someone inside. The door of the house opens. A shrunken man stands there. He's hunched over enough that you almost wish him some scaffolding. He takes a look at us. "No Girl Scout cookies for me. Awful sorry. I got the sugar. Can't eat that stuff anymore."

"We're not selling cookies. We're just neighbors—Petunia Posey's granddaughters. I'm Rae and this is Edie."

"We're cousins." I blurt, and immediately want to kick my own shin. I sound like I want a gold star for it or something.

The man looks at us and smiles. "Tuna's grands? I tell you *what*."

"*Tuna?*" The question comes out of both of us.

"Sorry, that was just an old nickname. She used to be one of the biggest fishes in the sea back when we were young." He stops himself. He puts his hand on his chest and looks from me to Rae. "Pardon me. Name's Zachary Amos, and I knew your grandmother well. I'm sorry for your loss. Come in, come in."

He steps back and motions us into the living area, which is a narrow space just inside the door. I hesitate, but Rae needs no encouragement. I follow her in. The air inside is chilly and loud from a window air conditioner, and it smells like baby powder and citrus fruits. "Hey, Mel!"

"Just a minute," an old woman's voice comes from somewhere inside. "We got company?"

"It's Tuna's grands," he calls out as he settles into a recliner and shoots the legs out with a loud *thwomp*. Rae and I sit on the edge of a couch.

"Tuna's?" this Mel lady calls back.

"That's right," he says.

Rae and I trade an amused look.

"We grew up together, Tuna and me," Zachary says. "Sure was sorry to learn of her passing."

Then a squeezy sound comes out of him, and I'm worried that he's crying. But he's not. He's laughing.

"My apologies, girls, my apologies," he says, trying to quiet his laugh. "It's just every time I think of when we were young—I always get to laughing." He looks up at us. "Well, you know, she always spoke her mind. *Always.* Even when we were real young. You probably know that."

"So we've heard." Rae smiles.

"Well, she was one of those who got her mouth washed out on a regular basis. Didn't even faze her. 'I prefer Ivory,' she'd say, like she's proud. 'None of that pink stuff.'"

Another laugh squeezes out of him, like he's telling a story he's forgotten could be funny. This time we both laugh with him.

"Tell them about the parade," the Mel voice calls from the other room.

"That's right," Zachary says. "She was driving a car when we were just ten years old. Youngest driver in the state—she wasn't worried about a license or anything. Drove a float in the Independence Day parade, back when this town was big enough to have those kind of shindigs."

"She did?" I ask, impressed.

"Sure did. She always did her own thing. Wore blue jeans to school, even. Doesn't sound like much to folks your age, but back then, it was against the rules."

So Petunia was a real rule breaker. *No wonder* she and my mom didn't get along!

"It sounds like you knew her pretty well," Rae says.

"I did. Think I even loved her once."

Rae and I must look intrigued, because Zachary says, "Oh, now, I think everyone was a little bit in love with Petunia, back then. But you know, she didn't quite love me back. Not the same way. My feelings for her? They was one-way. All out, no in."

"Unrequited?" Rae asks, making a sympathetic face.

"That's right. That's what it was."

From the short hallway, a woman walks into the room. She's wearing a yellow pantsuit and wedged sandals, and a gentle smile. Her hair is gray and curly, and slightly lopsided.

I realize she's wearing a wig, just slightly off center. It makes me feel a little sad, in a sweet way.

Zachary's whole *everything* changes when she walks into the room. He smiles, and his voice gets a little melodic. "Girls, meet my bride, Melba."

We both smile and greet her. Rae compliments Melba's pantsuit and Melba smiles and offers things—sandwiches, juice, grapefruits—all around. Rae and I both pass on it all, but Zachary takes her up on the offer. Before she slips back into the kitchen, she says, "Tell them about when she asked you to the stomp."

"What's a stomp?" Rae asks.

"Well, back in those days, it was a big to-do with a lot of dancing," he continues. "But this one in particular, it was the Flag Day stomp. This town sure has changed, but this was back in sixty-five." He leans back in his chair, his eyes focused on the wall above us. "That summer, I had my eye on her—well, lots of us fellows did. And *boy*, did she know it. I was working at the gas station. She pulled up in her daddy's new car—a Ford Galaxie. That's what it was. Red, like a maraschino cherry. A beauty. Both her and that car. And she said, 'Zachary Amos, I think you should take me to that stomp.'"

He stops and considers it, then breaks into a squeezy-sounding laugh. I'm reminded of the accordion bumper sticker.

"So I guess she kind of *told* me I was going to the stomp with her. She didn't ask me nothin'."

I feel a strike of admiration. Petunia was so bold! So *daring*!

Melba comes in with a small plate of cheese and crackers and a tiny glass of orange juice.

"Thank you, love," he says to her as he puts the plate down on a side table next to his chair. "Anyway, things didn't quite work out with us, but I have no regrets."

"So, did you end up going to the stomp together that night?" Rae asks.

"We did. But fact is, that's the night I met Melba. Didn't I, my dear?"

"You sure did," she says, and the two of them look at each other like we're not even in the room. I look away and notice the clock. The twins have been with Mitchell for almost half an hour.

I nudge Rae. "We should probably go."

Melba breaks her gaze away from her admiring husband and starts twittering about us having to go so soon, are we sure?

But as Zachary walks us toward the door, I realize something he said feels a little like a conversational cowlick: it sticks out to me, and I can't brush it away.

"So what happened that night at the stomp?"

He smiles and looks over at his wife. "I'm looking at her."

Melba laughs and waves her hands at his words. "All I did was march right up and ask him to dance, when Petunia was off being belle of the ball."

"It was the way you asked me. So sure of yourself," he says.

"Well, I *had* to be sure of myself. To look at me, I was just a lanky thing with Coke-bottle glasses and a metal contraption around my head to get my teeth straight."

"Maybe so, but just look at you *now*," he says, standing a little straighter, gazing into her eyes.

"Oh, sugar," she swoons back. "You are just too much."

Rae and I exchange little smiles. Then Rae says, "Well, thanks for having us in."

"You're welcome," Melba says. "It's kind of nice to talk about those old days at the Hurricane."

"The *Hurricane*?" I ask.

"That's right. The Hurricane. The old dance hall where you could really dance up a storm." She smiles. "That's what the sign used to say."

"And hoo boy, didn't we?" Zachary says. "Those were the days. Now it just sits there empty, jealous of the church on Sundays."

The old building. Across from the church. With the sign painted over.

Dance in the hurricane.

We quickly say our good-byes.

As we hurry back to the house, I muster some bravado. "Well, looks like we don't have to wait for a natural disaster to strike, then! I guess we know what we're doing tomorrow, even if we have to walk there. *Dance in the hurricane!* Item three is officially on the agenda!"

"*Edie,*" Rae says, tucking her chin. "Are you serious?"

"Of course I am," I say, feeling a little smug. Is she having doubts over whether we can pull it off? Could I even potentially out-brave Rae?

"I mean . . ." She laughs. "It's a *night*club. You don't go to a *night*club during the *day.*"

Ack! My smugness weakens into self-consciousness.

"Forget tomorrow," Rae says. "I know what we're doing *tonight.*"

Tonight? So soon? I start to feel the trademark surge of fear. "Oh, but . . ." There are many buts. But it's dark. But it's dangerous. But it's creepy. *But, but, but.*

"But what?"

I take in a big, brave, fear-conquering breath. A drive-the-car, jeans-to-school, I-prefer-Ivory breath.

"But let's be extremely quiet. If my mom catches us, we'll be locked in the study for the rest of the summer."

Chapter 9

Natural Disasters

Several hours later, when everyone's asleep, we *are* being extremely quiet—or trying to be. The floorboards creak as we creep down the hall and the stairs groan, but the sounds are disguised by all the other old-house noises: pipes pinging, the wind smacking branches into the roof, the eerie moan of the house as it settles down for the night.

The back door makes a horrible screech when we open it, and we both suck in a breath and stand as still as possible. My ears feel like they've suddenly become bionic. I listen for the squeak of a mattress as someone shifts in their bed, or some voices on alert, but the sound I hear is much smaller. A tiny grinding noise. A teensy gnawing.

Ack! So much for the peppermint-soaked cotton balls—our parents' first defense against the rodents. This is the sound of a feasting rat!

Rae and I look at each other and silently scream through gaping eyeballs. My fingers tingle with adrenaline as we scurry out the door and down the porch steps.

Outside, the air feels not so much alive, but *living*—a slow pulse, a warm breath, a watching eye. In the distance, frogs croak in unison and crickets chirp in that secret-army way.

There's a flash of light across the sky—heat lightning, they call it. For a single heartbeat, everything is as bright as day, and then, just as quickly, the sky is swallowed back up by the night.

We continue our scurry away from the house, with flashlights guiding our way. I'm afraid. Very afraid. *Tremendously* afraid. And I can't believe that I'm doing it anyway.

We're close enough that my arm brushes her. "You've got goose bumps," she whispers. "Scared?"

"Uh . . ." I hesitate. "Maybe?"

"I know, it's great, isn't it?"

While I marvel at her response, there's a swooping sound in the sky above us. Leaves rattle and branches sway in its wake, and I freeze. A bat! A witch! *Yikes!*

"That was probably an owl or something," Rae says.

Or something. I really wish she wouldn't say that. Let's just stick with *owl*. Definitely an owl. An adorable hooty little thing that's wise and kind, keeping us out of harm's way.

But what if ghosts are real? And what if Petunia is one of them? If she was, I tell myself, she probably wouldn't be the haunting type. She'd probably be whooping it up with Robin Williams, or dancing with Michael Jackson and Prince. Maybe even flying around with Amelia Earhart. The thought makes me feel a little better.

"Come on," Rae says. She sweeps her arms out and says, in a commanding voice, "'Let us step out into the night and pursue that flighty temptress, adventure!'"

I smile. This is one quote I know. "Dumbledore."

She grabs my hand, and we start to run through the grass. And somehow, just being connected to her makes me feel a little more fearless too. Maybe it's just that if we do come across something truly dangerous, I have a feeling she'll know what to do, the same way she knows coffee and cinematic masterpieces and witty banter. Fear starts to fade a little—just a little—into the background, second to the exhilaration of running through the tall grass, late at night, attached to my cousin.

One flickering streetlight illuminates the cracked asphalt lot surrounding the big abandoned building, which looks particularly frightening at night. We may be at the Hurricane, but there's no hint of "dancing up a storm" here. If anything, it looks like a storm has passed through—an actual natural disaster. The air smells dank and sour, like the smell of an old skunk.

There's a NO TRESPASSING sign hanging sideways off the door of the building, which is locked tightly with a chain. Neither the sign nor the security measure seems necessary—no one in their right mind would want to get into this building. Well, no one except Rae, who is trying her hardest to pry open a window.

As much as I try to channel the New Edie, this is feeling less like a fear-conquering adventure and more like a criminal act. "Um, Rae, what if there's an alarm system?"

"There's no alarm system," she says, so certain.

A pair of headlights beams in our direction, from down the road. "Oh, no! Run!" I say, and duck around the corner of the building.

"Edie!" she whisper-scolds.

The car passes by. "Next time, don't panic, Edie. If you stay still, no one's going to see us. Just relax."

I don't point out that it's impossible to relax when you're crouched beside a decaying building in the middle of the night, and your heart is beating so hard and fast that you can feel it in your toenails. In fact, it's amazing that the whole town can't hear it.

Rae walks over to another window and surveys it with her flashlight. The glass is slightly crooked, so there's a small gap under one edge. "Awesome," she says. But it looks a little high to reach easily. "Give me a boost."

"Rae? I'm not sure this is such a good idea anymore."

"We made it this far. I'm not about to just go home *now*."

I guess I don't look too convinced, because she adds, "Come on, Edie. I thought you had a sense of adventure!"

Which I do. I do! *I DO!* And I'm determined to prove it!

I crouch down on a knee in the sandy dirt and lace my fingers together to make a place for her foot. Rae steps into it and I boost her up. I hear her grunting and feel her tugging away as she tries to pry the window open. Just before my palms are ready to give way, she says, "Push me higher!"

I try to summon a surge of energy, but my hands collapse in pain, and she lands back on the sandy ground with me.

"Sorry," I say, shaking my hands out. I look up at the window, which she's managed to open just a few more inches. "But I'm not sure we're going to be able to squeeze through there."

"You're not chickening out, are you?"

"No!" I stand up, dusting myself off, determined not to let this item from Petunia's list slip away. I need a checkmark! "I'm saying maybe we need to find another way."

Despite the stubborn urge to run in the opposite direction, I start toward the back of the building with Rae. A rear door there is chained shut, like the front entrance, but looser. Rae pulls at it. "There's some slack in this chain," she says. "I bet we can get in if we suck in our breath."

I make myself smile. "After you."

She draws in a deep breath and starts to wiggle sideways into the building. "Holy crap, it's dark in there," she says, halfway in. But it doesn't stop her. She continues to shimmy through. Once she's in, she says, "Hurry up! It's kind of creepy in here without you."

Without you. Her words are like fuel. I pull in my stomach and squeeze and scrape though the small opening. I meet her just inside the door, under the red glow of the exit light, and we grab hands and both laugh nervously. Even though this place feels dead—dark, still, and eerily quiet—I feel incredibly alive. I'm aware of every nerve in my body, every beat of my heart, every hair on the back of my neck.

Despite our flashlights, it's too dark to see much inside the building. Then I get an idea. "If the exit light works, there must still be electricity in the building." I beam my flashlight across the walls and spot a switch panel, just behind us. I start flipping switches until the lights come on, exposing a vast empty space. The floors are dark and dusty. Wood beams cross just below the peaked ceiling. In the center of the room, a large crystal chandelier lights up with a soft glow.

Rae looks pleased. She hands me her phone. "Now for a photo opp."

She stands under the chandelier, smiles, and poses, hand on a hip.

"Do the hip-bump thing," I say. "Like you do with that chicken in the commercial."

"That's ridiculous," she says. But she makes a goofy face and sweeps her arms to the left and her hips to the right. I snap a photo and hand the phone back to her.

She looks at it and laughs. "Oh, my god. I look like *such* an idiot. Redo! We definitely need a beat." She finds some music on her phone, a vaguely familiar song with a catchy, thumping bass line. "Okay, Edie, here's how dancing in the hurricane is done."

She closes her eyes and starts to move to the electronic pulse, first bobbing her head from side to side. She bites her bottom lip under her front teeth and then starts sidestepping with wide strides, her hips and arms drawing wobbly circles. It doesn't exactly look coordinated.

I really don't think she'd want me to snap a picture of *that*.

Her eyes flip open, and she notices I'm standing still. Watching her.

"Come on, Edie. Dance! *Dance!*"

"Oh, but your photo—"

"Don't worry about that now. Just dance!"

"I'm the world's worst dancer," I tell her.

She starts doing some sort of wide-stance crouching move. And then she's jumping, punching the air.

"You can't be," Rae says.

And she's right. Because with her moves, my cousin, my perfect cousin, could easily be mistaken for an all-out dork. And she doesn't seem to care. Not a single bit.

She laughs and dances—well, flails—a little closer to me. "Edie! Dance!" She is moving like some sort of rusted machine. "See what I mean? It's me. *I'm* the world's worst dancer."

I promise to start dancing the minute I can. But it's hard to move when I'm laughing this hard—I'm gasping for air! She is twirling, strutting, and *not even caring* under the glow of the grand chandelier, to the thump of the music. She is thrashing, spinning, basking in the swirl of red party lights.

Hold on. *A swirl of red party lights?*

My gaze jerks toward the back door, and a blast of cold panic streaks through my body. My laugh gets gargled in my throat. The chain hangs, the door is completely ajar. A bright light is aimed right at us. Rae suddenly stops dancing. We frantically reach for each other and squeeze ourselves together tight.

Just outside the door, a dark figure stands watching.

Chapter 10

Storm Warning

Just outside the back door of the Hurricane, the figure steps closer.

I hear a shrill sound before I recognize it as my own scream. I am yanked away from the door, pulled toward the inched-open window, by Rae's strong grip.

"Don't be scared," a man's drawly voice says.

Which is, of course, what any serial killer might say to his prey. It just makes us scramble faster. The two of us frantically try to pry open the window, our one hope for escape.

"Friends—"

I hear a burst of static, followed by a woman's voice breaking through. "E-twenty-two, copy detail."

"E-twenty-two, present. Hello, Nora."

This dark figure is a policeman, not a killer! I feel a flood of relief. But it doesn't have the same effect on Rae.

"A cop! We gotta get out of here! Now!" Rae almost shouts. But the window's still not budging.

"E-twenty-two, we have a three-nine-three off the three-eleven."

His radio crackles again, and the voice says, "You said a *three-nine-three*?"

"Sure did. Off the three-eleven."

"Well, I'm onsite now. More of a one-eleven here." He chuckles.

"Step back, Edie. I'm going to break it!"

"*Oh*, I wouldn't do that if I were you. Don't want to have to give you a vandalism charge on top of breaking and entering," the policeman says. "Now, I need you both to turn around and face me."

Rae and I look at each other. She looks as defeated as I feel. We turn around slowly, joining hands again.

"Officer George Elwayne, officer of the peace," he says. Now that I can see him better, I see he's a short, gray-haired older man with a ponytail. Still, I'm terrified—now about how much trouble we're in. "So, friends, who, may I ask, are you?"

We both hesitate to answer.

The staticky voice breaks back in. "You need any backup?"

He looks at us. "Girls? You about to tell me who you are, or do I need to ask for backup?"

"Rae Posey," she answers in a sullen tone.

"Edith Posey-Preston," I answer.

"Of the Petunia Poseys?" he asks.

We nod.

"That might explain it."

"Elwayne?" the static voice says.

"No backup—I got it," he says into his button. To us, he says, "Just what are you girls doing in here?"

"We were just . . . looking around," Rae says.

"Unless you're looking for trouble, I'd say you're in the wrong place." He sighs and shakes his head. "Now, into the patrol car."

"The police car? Why?" Rae asks.

His head wobbles a little. "Because, well . . . you girls know what *condemned* means?"

Oh my god! Condemned! Sentenced to punishment! What have we done? Petunia's list really *is* a list of bad ideas! My eyes start to sting. "What exactly are we—" I swallow. I try to be brave and face it. "What exactly are we . . . *condemned* to?"

"Now, Edith, is it?"

"Edie," I say, although I don't feel so Edie-like at the moment.

"Well, Edie, I'm taking you girls home to your parents.

It's the *building* that's condemned. That means it's unsafe. You could get hurt in here."

Oh. That kind of condemned. Still this is the last thing my mom needs to hear!

"Can you please not tell our parents? Please?" I beg.

He sighs. "Look, friends. Let's all take a deep breath together, okay? Three counts in, four counts out."

We look at him.

"Come on, all together!" he commands, circling his hand in front of him. It feels strange to do it, but we try to breathe along with him. It takes great effort.

After a not-so-relaxing exhale, I say, "We were really just exploring. We didn't mean to break the law! We're really sorry, and—"

"It won't happen again," Rae says.

"Glad to hear," he says, though it doesn't seem to make a difference. "Now . . ." He sweeps his arms in the direction of the patrol car. "Into the car, both of you."

We trudge outside, and Rae and I slide into the backseat of Officer Elwayne's patrol car. I feel like I'm on the brink of tears.

"Well, Houston, we have a problem," Rae says quietly.

For a second, I'm a little lost. Houston?

"*Apollo 13*, Edie. The movie?" She shakes her head. "I just mean this sucks."

"I know," I say, thinking about what my mom will do.

Rae continues. "I mean, we never got any great shots in there. And just look at this one—I look like such a dweeb!" She shows me her phone screen—the photo I took of her inside the Hurricane.

That's her biggest concern?

"Aren't you worried about what our parents are going to do?" I ask.

"I don't care about missing dessert for a week."

"Missing dessert for a week? That's all your dad will do?"

"Okay, maybe two weeks. Why?"

I look at her. "Because I'm going to be grounded for the rest of the summer."

She smirks.

"I'm not joking."

Officer Elwayne gets into the driver's seat and turns off the swirling lights. "So," he says. "Awful sorry about your grandmother."

"Thanks," we both say.

"Now, Rae and Edie, right? Which one of you's Hannah's girl?"

"I am," I say.

He glances at me in the rearview mirror. "Well, *well*," he says with a soft laugh. "My old friend Hannah."

"You know her?" I ask.

"Yep. Used to."

We pull up in front of the house. It looks so quiet, so convincingly peaceful, it almost feels believable that Officer Elwayne would just give us a little wink and tell us that, on second thought, he'd rather not wake anyone up and alarm them.

But no such luck.

We're in the parlor—Rae and me, and our parents. Mercifully, when Officer Elwayne delivered us to them, he kindly left off the whole breaking-and-entering part of this evening, but our parents are all still reeling over the fact that we were found wandering outside in the middle of the night. They are also blatantly disregarding Officer Elwayne's advice to "center" themselves and calm down with deep breaths (three counts in, four counts out).

Rae and I are huddled on the couch as my mom paces in front of us. Her robe is cinched tight; her face has a matching expression.

"What on earth has come over you, Edith?"

I shrug.

My dad scratches his head. "Well, there must be some reason you were sneaking out at night."

"Yes, Edith. It just doesn't seem like you. Do you care to offer any explanation?"

Even though I feel a quick stab of guilt, I don't really want to tell her about the list. She'd rule it out for us, on the basis that it violates several rules of sensibility, practicality, and safety. Which it does, *gloriously* so.

Uncle A.J. looks as serious as I've ever seen him. "Was this your idea, Rae?"

"No!"

"Well, I don't know what's going on, but I think there should be some real consequences," my mom says, the creases in her forehead deepening.

"I couldn't agree more," Uncle A.J. says. "Rae, you're not leaving this house tomorrow."

Rae makes a face at her dad.

"Tomorrow?" My mom scoffs. "Well, Edith is grounded indefinitely. No more leaving the house without a parent, period."

"You know what, Rae?" Uncle A.J. says. "I hope you enjoyed your outing, because you're grounded indefinitely too!"

"Dad! That's ridiculous!"

He seems to hesitate, but my mom places her hand on his shoulder and sends us upstairs.

We're finally in our beds.

"I'm sorry about my mom," I say to Rae. "Sorry we're grounded."

"I know," she says.

"She can be so *annoying*," I say.

"Edie, I'm *sooo* tired."

"Oh. Yeah, me too."

"So, talk tomorrow, okay?"

"All right." I adjust my pillow. I try to close my eyes. Even though I am tired, they keep trying to pop open.

"But Rae?"

"Hmm?"

"Thanks for doing that with me. Even though we got in trouble, I had fun."

"Yeah. And even though I didn't get a good picture to post, it was pretty awesome," she says.

I start to smile. I might not have actually danced in the Hurricane, but . . . I laugh. "I can't believe we snuck out."

"We *totally* did."

"And we really broke into an abandoned building?"

"The dynamic duo can do anything!" Rae says, meaning me and her. Her and me. Us.

"And we survived it all!" I beam.

"Seriously!" Rae laughs. "Tonight was *epic*."

She yawns loudly, and I yawn too. I don't remember being so exhausted—*ever*. But even though my body wants to shut down, my brain won't cooperate. It's filling up with thoughts, marinating in feelings. Guilt. Thrill. Pride. And mostly excitement. Because when Taylor calls me on visiting day, two weeks from now, I can tell her all about it. Take that, Sophi Angelo!

And I realize that even though I'm practically grounded forever, I'm starting to feel a little free.

Chapter 11

Likes

As added punishment to being grounded, our workload has increased tenfold over the last couple days. Today we're sentenced to weeding the garden. My mother has given us gloves, sunscreen, water, some old beach towels to lay under our knees, and lots and lots of safety instructions. The air is hot and sticky, the sun is searing, and I have a feeling that time is stuck like an ant in a drop of glue.

We're moving in slow motion. Rae grabs a handful of something and pulls it out of the ground. "Is this a plant or a weed?" she asks, holding it up.

"Plant. I think?" Although it's too late for this one.

I wipe the sweat off my forehead, and Rae groans and

flops down. "Being grounded sucks."

"Yeah," I say. "But it was worth it."

"Speaking of . . ." She pulls her phone out of her pocket. "Oh my god, Edie! In just two days I'm up to two hundred and forty-nine likes on that dorky photo at the Hurricane! I honestly can't believe it!" She smiles big. "Yeah, I guess it was pretty worth it!"

I smile back, but in the back of my mind, I wonder if it would have still been worth it to her if she didn't have as many likes. I turn back to the weeds. At least weeds are easy to understand. *Wait—weed or plant?* Weed. No, definitely plant. Well, okay, eas*ier* to understand.

After I pull a few more green things from the ground, I notice I've pretty much been working solo for a while. I look over my shoulder. She's lying on a beach towel, texting away.

"Sorry, Edie, I'll help in a second, okay?" Then she holds the phone at arm's length and says, in her classic-movie voice, "I'm ready for my close-up." She snaps a selfie.

"Rae." I smile. "What on earth are you doing?"

"Just working."

"Um—"

"I mean, that's my caption. 'Hard at work.' You know, lounging here on this beach towel." She smiles, her eyes glued to her phone screen. "I'm texting this one to Vivian. One of my beasties."

"Your *beasties*?"

"I'm kidding. My besties, of course."

She sends her message and finally puts her phone down. "You look exhausted. Maybe we should look into the child labor laws. We might actually have a case."

We hear excited voices coming from the backyard. I take a peek around the corner of the house.

"Did you know the Komodo dragon kills its victims by infecting it with its mouth germs?" It's Beatrice.

"*Yeah*, and when they kill something, the dragon babies roll around in the prey's guts so that they stink as much as possible and no animal will want to come near them." That's Henry.

The twins are practically clamoring around Mitchell as he tries to make his way to the snakes. "No, I didn't know any of that," Mitchell says, "But thank you. That's . . . uh . . . good stuff."

"Hey, *Edie*. You've practically memorized Petunia's list. What's the next thing on it?"

"You mean item four?" It's another thing that feels pretty out of reach, especially since I'm the kind of person who has to have imaginary boyfriends. "It's 'master flirting.'"

But when I look over at her, she gives me a slow smile that says she already knew the answer. "So I'd say maybe today's a good day to check that box. With Snake Boy."

"Well, I—I," I stammer, a little flustered. "I don't even . . . know him, really."

"Maybe you'd like to get to know him *a little better*," she says in a syrupy, teasing voice.

I try to laugh, but my breath comes out in little frantic bursts.

"Uh-oh, I think you like him," Rae says, almost singing. "You really like him."

"What? No—no, I do *not*, Rae. I mean, not like *that*."

"Okay, fine. You don't like him like *that*. That doesn't mean you can't flirt with him."

I bite my bottom lip. I *do* want that checkmark. "There's this guy down here—he's cute, with turquoise eyes, and very mysterious, and we sort of have a thing," I'll tell Taylor when she calls. And she'll realize how exciting I am now, how far I've come since this past spring, when I chickened out and played sick the whole week the class was paired off for square dancing in P.E.

"So what would I even do?" I ask.

"Just talk to him," she says, like it's all so easy. Which for her, I'm sure, it is.

"About what?"

"I don't know, Edie—about anything. It's not so much what you say, it's how you say it."

Like that helps.

I study him. He's just another weird kid, like me, right? Nothing to be too nervous about. Maybe I can just march over there and talk to him—about what, though? Snakes? Frogs? Reptiles? Ugh.

Rae follows my glance. "Okay, I was totally joking, but you do—"

"No, *I do not.*" And then I say, "Anyway, I have a boyfriend," mostly so she'll stop teasing me about Mitchell.

But she doesn't. "Well, the way you're looking at Snake Boy, I kind of feel sorry for Klaus."

I hear Beatrice's voice again. It's like someone turned her volume up a few notches. "Hey, Mitchell! Did you know the largest snake in the world is the reticulated python?"

Then Henry's words pour out quickly, and even louder. "Yeah, and it grows to about twenty-five feet long! And did you know the most poisonous reptile is a poison arrow frog? Just a drop of its poison can kill a bunch of people—"

"Well," I say, grateful for the distraction, "the only person you should feel sorry for right now is Mitchell. It's an SOS situation. The supertwins are on full attack."

We go into the backyard, and Rae calls out, "Never fear, Mitchell. We're here to save you!" Then she runs across the lawn, toward the snake enclosures. "The dynamic duo to the rescue!"

But I'm not feeling too dynamic at the moment, and I'm not sure if it's the thought of the snakes or the boy *with* them that's making me so skittish.

I take a breath. I can do this, right? I allow myself to fall forward, one leg at a time. From the outside, it must look like running. I make it about halfway through the yard, halfway to the serpents' lair, before my run slows to a reluctant walk.

Rae's made it over to Henry. She taps him on the shoulder and runs a few steps away.

"Yes?" he asks her.

"Henry, I just tagged you. You're it!"

"It?"

"Yeah." She laughs. "Come on, you're supposed to try to tag me back."

"Oh, *it*. We don't play it."

"It's called *tag*," Rae says, laughing. "So what were you playing with Colvin the other day?"

"Oh, that was fetch," Beatrice says. "And Colvin was pretty good at it, even though he's just a human and not a dog."

Rae stops and looks over at me. "Okay, wow. Rescuing Mitchell from these dizygotes is going to be harder than I thought."

I walk a little closer to them. Every inch feels like a mile. "Come on, you guys. Leave Mitchell alone."

"Why?" Henry asks.

"He's trying to clean out the cages. You're probably driving him crazy. Just go play. And not fetch."

Beatrice looks at me. "Then what?"

I give Rae a please-help look.

"All right, supertwins, show me something smart," Rae says.

Beatrice looks suddenly excited. "Oh, oh, Henry! Let's show her *our* way of measuring trees."

Henry races her to the line of trees at the edge of the yard, and Rae follows them. I am alone with Mitchell. I get a fluttering attack of the nerves, but I just try to smile and cross my arms in some easy-looking way. And avoid his eyes at all costs.

"So," he says, "you don't much like them, do you? Snakes."

"Oh." I gust-laugh. "Is it that obvious?"

He gives a little shrug. "Well, you seem nervous."

"I'm working on it. I'll get over it, I will." I exhale. "Eventually."

"Well, you can start by coming closer. I promise I won't let any loose." He puts a few handfuls of shredded paper on the bottom of an enclosure.

I try to take another step, but my feet don't want to work with me. "Hey, Mitchell?"

"Yeah?"

"What about snakes in the grass?" I ask.

He looks at me like I'm speaking a different language.

"I mean, well, say, you were walking around outside in the yard or the grass or something, and you wanted to make sure that if there are any snakes nearby, they know you're coming. So they have a chance to, you know—"

"You mean slither away?"

Slither. The word itself gives me chills. "Yeah, I guess—"

But our conversation is interrupted by Beatrice. "Edith! This tree's forty-five feet tall!"

I shade my eyes and squint. I see that Rae and Henry are bent over, in wide stances. From where their heads touch the ground, they are looking up at the trees. Beatrice is taking slow, exacting steps from the tree toward them.

Mitchell's voice is slow, confused. "Uh, what are they . . . ?"

"Oh. If you can see the top of the tree from ground level, you're about as far away as it is tall. It assumes a forty-five degree angle from the ground, where your head is, to the tree top." I explain. "It's just practical trigonometry."

He smiles. Okay, he *dimples.*

Even though he seems a little impressed, like he thinks I'm kind of smart, I'm feeling pretty dumb because of the goofy, supersized smile that I can't seem to wipe off my face. My eyes start to seek his out, but I catch them doing that and force myself to look away and watch Rae and the twins.

It looks like she's started teaching them to play tag after all.

But then Mitchell says, "You know, you can always make kissing noises."

"Uh—" *Kissing noises?* I don't know what he's talking about, but I feel suddenly sunburned with embarrassment.

"To scare away the snakes, if there are any around. Just make kissing sounds. Scares them off."

I feel a nervous laugh start to erupt, but I know how *that* works around him. I will turn into some sort of snort-snot machine, so I just give him a smile and walk off—okay, *kiss* off—to join Rae and the twins. No wonder I have to make up boyfriends. I couldn't flirt my way out of my own underwear drawer.

Henry squeals and runs. It looks like Rae just became it. And tag's a much easier game than this flirting thing anyway.

Later, Rae and I are in our room. I've just finished brushing my teeth, and she's just finished a heavy texting session with Leo. She lets out a happy sigh, and then in a nasally monotone she says, "E.T. phone home." She pushes the phone into my hand.

"Oh, but—"

"Just text him already!" She's talking about Klaus.

"I think I'm too tired."

"Oh-*kay*." She takes the phone back and reclines on her bed. "Suit yourself. But don't you miss him?"

I try to smile, but it feels more like a grimace. "I don't know, Rae. I don't think we're like you and Leo." *As, well, one of us isn't even real.*

She glances over. "What do you mean?"

"Oh, well . . . I guess I don't really feel like we need to stay in touch all the time."

"I bet I know why," she says. Her voice has this sweet and gooey tone to it.

"Why?" I ask, feeling a little nervous.

She props herself up on her elbow. "I bet it's because you haven't kissed Klaus."

I almost wince at the thought of having lip-to-lip contact with this imaginary boyfriend. "Well, no." *Lederhosen! Knee socks!* "I haven't."

"Well, just wait till you do," she says. "That changes everything."

"What's it like?" I ask. I can't help myself.

"It's just *amazing*," she says, snapping off the light. I hear her yawn.

"Amazing *how*?"

"It's like, oh, I don't know . . ." Her voice gets kind of dreamy and floaty sounding. "Your mouth is being squeezed by a vacuum."

"A vacuum?"

"Well, like between pillows in a vacuum. I mean"—the dreamy/floaty tone leaving her voice—"it's hard to explain. One day you'll understand." And then she sort of giggles. "Hey, Edie. Maybe *you'll* be the one to kiss the charmer."

"Oh, uh." I laugh. Panic starts to simmer quietly inside of me. I'm clearly not capable of flirting with a boy—I can't even imagine kissing one!

But Rae's right about the comment she made earlier today: I *have* memorized Petunia's list of good ideas. I say, "Well, that's the last thing on the list." So, thankfully, there's a lot to do before I have to face it.

Chapter 12

Dirty Laundry

"Hey, Edith," says a supertwin. "Mom says to get up."

I keep my eyes closed.

I feel Beatrice shake my shoulder. "Edith. Wake up."

"I'm awake," I mumble.

Snickering.

I am aware of something close to my face. I open one eye. A glassy-eyed, gray-and-black creature stares down at me.

I yank myself up, toppling over Albert/Odysseus. The twins break into fits of laughter. "Ha *ha*. You guys are *so* funny," I say. "Now will you please leave me alone!?"

"But Mom *did* say to wake you up," Beatrice says.

"And take Albert with you!"

"His name," Beatrice says, "is Odysseus."

I throw my pillow in their general direction and they scatter out of the room, leaving me alone with the stuffed dog. I put on my glasses and look over at him. His vacant blue eyes stare back at me. Maybe Albert/Odysseus isn't so bad. I reach up and pet him. I wonder where Rae is.

"You *do* like him!" Beatrice says, giggling. The twins haven't made it very far. They're peering in from the hallway.

"Don't you guys have an extinct bird to find?" I ask.

"It's endangered. No one can find an *extinct* bird," Henry says.

"I *know* that, Henry. Now go somewhere else, you guys. I need some privacy."

"You're no fun anymore," I hear Beatrice say, but at least I get the intended effect. They leave, shutting—okay, slamming—my door behind them. I hear their footsteps finally making their way down the hall.

I stand up, slip on a clean T-shirt and some clean-enough shorts, and go downstairs. Rae's sitting at the table drinking her morning coffee as my mother sorts through the mail.

"Hi," I say.

"Morning, honey," my mom says.

"Hey, sleepyhead," Rae says.

The phone rings, and I lunge for it. *Taylor? Could it be?*

133

Already? Could she be home from camp early? Bored with Sophi, missing me? "Hello?"

"Good morning. This is the Polk County Animal Shelter. Could I speak to an adult?"

I slump and hand the phone over to my mother.

"Expecting a call?" Rae jokes. She mouths the words, "From Klaus?"

My eyes go wide with panic. My mom seems to be happily chatting away on the phone, but still—she's less than ten feet away! I'd be mortified if she knew anything about a boyfriend, real or otherwise!

My mom hangs up the phone and announces, "The animal shelter is doing a clothing drive. They're picking up donations tomorrow. This sounds like a good job for you girls. Petunia's got a whole closet full of things that will be as good as new after a good wash."

"Great. Laundry day." I groan.

But just as I try to secretly scavenge for a Pop-Tart, a stream of water starts pouring in through the ceiling above the sink. My dad clomps down the stairs and rushes into the kitchen. *"Oh, dragonfly droppings!"*

"Walter! What's the matter?"

"Maybe my aim's a little off these days," he says.

Then Uncle A.J. stomps down the stairs, shouting out things that horrify my mom. As they start to argue, Rae turns to me. "Hey, Edie," she says in an extra-quiet voice. "No worries, okay? I won't tell your parents. I can keep a secret."

A secret?

"About Klaus." She gestures zipping her lips shut. "I totally get it. My dad doesn't know about Leo either. Well, he *knows* Leo. He just doesn't know that he's my *boyfriend*."

We exchange a conspiratorial smile. I feel a little guilty about lying, but I have to admit—I like this feeling of approval. If I can be exciting enough for *Rae*, this adventurous almost-famous cousin of mine, then hanging on to Taylor seems a little more possible.

Uncle A.J. makes it jarringly clear that the *bleeping* water will have to be shut off, and my mother says, "A.J., will you please watch your mouth?"

"I don't *have to*, with you doing it for me!"

He dashes outside, and we hear the crank of a rusty water valve turning.

"Well, so much for laundry. *And* sanity," my mom says. "Walt, maybe we should think about buying a new refrigerator. I know this one's really going."

"A refrigerator?" my dad asks.

"You could be *really* helpful by pioneering that effort," she says to him, giving him a wide smile. "Girls, I guess you're on mildew duty today. We'll just have to do a clothing donation another time."

"Aunt Hannah?" Rae asks. "There's a Laundromat downtown. We drive past it on the way to the diner. Maybe Edie and I can wash the clothes there and get them ready for the pickup."

"A Laundromat? Rae, how do you know how to . . ." My mom's sentence slows to a halt.

"I'll be *thirteen* in October. I've been doing laundry since I was ten."

I'm amazed at her range of talents, her scope of skill. She's so smart—not like the Posey-Preston book-sponge kind of smart, but the real-life kind of smart. So *capable*.

"Well, if I'm supposed to be looking at refrigerators, maybe I can drop the girls off on my way to Home Depot," my dad suggests.

My mom tilts her head. "Okay, girls, start collecting Petunia's clothes, then. But I'd like to remind you that you're in town to do laundry. None of this wandering around. Understood?"

"We understand," Rae says. With a smile that makes me wonder what she's planning.

My dad makes his thinking noises as he drives us downtown. It sounds like he's trying to suck something out of his teeth. "A refrigerator," he says. "Never bought one before, but it can't be that hard, right?"

"You should get a stainless steel one," Rae says. "With that little button you can press for ice. It's so hot down here."

We pull up in front of the Laundromat. "Be back in . . . what do they say around here? Two shakes of a coon's tail?"

"Dad, they don't say that down here. Or probably anywhere," I say as we get out of the car.

"Yeah, Uncle Walt. All the reptiles probably ate all of the raccoons anyway."

Rae and I go inside with our quarters and three bags of Petunia's clothes, a large number of them zebra patterned, tiger striped, and leopard spotted. The place is empty, so we fill up three washers and Rae adds detergent. She gives me a handful of quarters, but I'm not sure what to do with them. I watch as she slides them into slots and presses the plate in. There's the sound of water filling the washer. Is there nothing this girl can't do?

"All right, Edie." Rae surveys the place. "I'm seeing a lot of possibilities."

"For what, exactly?" Because in an empty Laundromat in a tiny town, there don't seem to be a lot of possibilities for much of anything.

"For likes." She tosses her phone to me and goes over to the double-stacked row of dryers. "Okay, when I say *when*, take a picture." She opens a dryer door on the top row, takes hold of the rim, and launches up and into it, so that only her legs dangle frantically. I can't help but laugh a little—she does look ridiculous. "When!" she calls, and I snap the photo.

She climbs down from the dryer and commends me on my photo. "Post," she says as she presses a few buttons on her phone. "Okay, what next? I'd say you should try flirting again, but well, look around." She does a drawly impression of Officer Elwayne—"Unless you've got your heart set on some fabric softener, I'd say you're out of luck."

I give her a little smile. "I actually might have better luck with that fabric softener."

She laughs.

"I'm sort of serious."

"Flirting's not that hard, Edie. I think you're overanalyzing it."

"You do?"

"Either that or you really *do* like Mitchell, so you get all jittery—"

"It's not that!"

She looks at me. "Okay, good. Because actually, I think Mitchell's the perfect person for someone trying to master their skills."

"You do?"

"Yeah," she says. "He's basically pretty nice, so he's never going to make you feel completely stupid. And he's just okay looking, so you're not like, 'Oh my god, he's talking to me!'"

Maybe I should feel a little offended on his behalf, but I don't—in fact, I'm relieved. She doesn't like him like that. Could there be hope for me?

"Okay, so . . . how do I not overanalyze it?"

"Well, this is a no-brainer, but for one, it's mostly about eye contact."

"Uh. Can you be more specific?"

"See? You *are* overanalyzing!"

"I'm not sure I know how not to," I admit.

She sighs. "All right, fine. Let's overanalyze it then."

She turns me to face her and signals me to look directly at her eyes. "Okay, not like this . . ." Her brown eyes go wide. "And not like this . . ." Now she makes them into slivers. "But more like this." She tilts her head and lets her eyelids drop a little.

It makes her look sort of tired, but I don't tell her that.

She continues. "And keep looking at him like that for like an extra second too long. Like a second past 'I'm listening to you,' and a second *before* 'I'm a stalker and you should be very afraid.'"

"Oh. Okay," I say, even though I'm possibly more confused than ever.

"You should also find out what you have in common with him—if there's something you both like to do, then maybe you can do it together."

I wonder what that could be with Mitchell. And I probably will *continue* to wonder. I sigh.

"It also helps to have something to give him," Rae adds.

"Wait, so now I have to *bring a present*?"

"I just mean, give him *something*. Gum is good. Tic Tacs are good too. Although sometimes that backfires because he might think you're telling him his breath stinks. I don't know, Edie. Just something. But whatever it is, just be casual about it."

"Okay, Tic Tacs, things in common, eye contact—"

"And don't forget to make him laugh."

I probably give him plenty to laugh *at*. It's the laugh-*with* thing that's the problem. I just say, "Oh."

"You know what I do, Edie? If I can't think of something funny to say, sometimes I just give Leo a sort of hard time about whatever. Like joke with him, you know?" She looks at my face. "Okay, would an example help?"

I nod.

"Okay, like once, Leo totally blew his line. He was like, 'What light through yonder window breaks? It is the *west*, and Juliet is the sun.' Can you believe it? You don't even have to know Shakespeare to know it's *east*. So, anyway, it was pretty funny, so I always give him a hard time about it."

"Huh."

The washers slow their spinning. Rae gets up to start

loading the clothes into the dryers. "So does that make any more sense, Edie?"

"I . . . guess so," I say, though I still feel pretty clueless.

She lines up the quarters in the change slot and closes the last dryer. "Now I have a question for you." She glances over at me. "How'd you get a boyfriend if you don't know how to flirt?"

My mouth opens, though my mind goes suddenly blank.

"Wait—let me guess. Chess club."

That'll work. "How'd you know?"

She shrugs. "That's where all the smart kids go. But think about it this way: if you can master chess, you can master flirting. It's just another game."

I can't help but admire her. Nothing seems to scare her. It's almost like she doesn't believe in fear—like she thinks it's something that belongs in the same category as the tooth fairy.

I try to ask my next question casually. "Do you ever get nervous? Around boys?"

"I guess so. But if I let *nervous* get to me every time I felt it, I could never get up onstage. You know my philosophy, Edie. *Carpe diem!*"

I look up at her, hoping she'll elaborate a little more about this nervousness and how to get through it. Because everything I've done so far this summer—or actually not done, as the case may be—has involved her. And flirting . . . well, she can't flirt *for* me, can she?

But she says, "And you know what? Speaking of carpe-ing the diem, I think it's a great day for ice cream."

I know we're not supposed to be wandering around town. But I look out the window. It's a straight shot across the street to Augustus Tools and Treats, so I think we can get there without any meandering.

When we arrive at the shop, Welles greets us with two tall glasses of ice water.

His ma nods at us from behind the counter as we sit down. "Nuts," she says.

"These girls are not *nuts*, Ma," he says, looking up at the ceiling.

"Well, did they bring us any?"

"Now *why* would they bring us nuts, Ma?"

The bell jingles on the door. A tall, leathery-skinned woman walks in and waves to Welles. "Just in for a few cool breaths. That heat'll make you madder than a bobcat."

"Hey there, Rosie," Welles says. He pours a third glass of water and slides it across the counter to her. "Another gator sighting today?"

Rae and I raise our eyebrows at each other.

"Yep. A call from a passerby. Said she saw a gator over

there by the Buy 'n' Tote. Can you even imagine? But when I got there, *nada*, hear me? *Not a* darn thing."

The woman nods at Rae and me and reaches out her hand. "Rosie Dunwoody, pleased to meet you."

"Rosie, these are Petunia Posey's grands, Rae and Edie," Welles says.

"A smart woman, Petunia Posey," Rosie says. "Sorry for your loss."

We give her some words of thanks, and Welles says, "Girls, Rosie's our go-to gator woman. She wrangles any gators we find around town."

"You're an alligator wrangler?" Rae sounds as impressed as I feel.

"Well, a trapper. But, sure, wrangler sounds better. I just take alligators out of the places they shouldn't be—backyards, pools, playgrounds—and put them back into the wild where they belong." She looks at my face and then laughs. "Now, don't let that get to you. We don't have a lot of them around these parts. But there have been more calls than usual lately. Except there's no alligator to be found."

"I saw one of them good-for-nothin' swamp critters last night," Welles's ma pipes up from behind her tiny television screen.

Rosie and Welles exchange a knowing smile, and Welles says, "Oh, yeah? Where was that, Ma?"

"Was on my front porch. Sittin' there, under the swing."

"That so?" Welles looks like he's fighting a smile. "And what did you do about it, Ma?"

"It looked hungry. I gave it some roast beef," she grumbles.

"Well, Ma, I'm sure that nasty swamp critter appreciated you sharing your dinner."

"No, sir, it did *not*! Left it there for the flies. That's the last time—"

It takes a lot of effort for us not to laugh too loudly. Rosie manages to say, "Well, Mrs. Augustus, next time you spot a gator on your porch, you give Elwayne a call."

But Welles's ma holds up her hand to signal she's done talking—her "stories" just came back on.

"So how many alligators *have* you caught?" Rae asks Rosie.

"Hard to say. After twenty years or so, you stop counting."

"Have you ever gotten bitten?" I ask.

"Sure I have—it comes with the territory. Nothing so bad it hasn't healed."

"But don't you get . . . scared?" I mean, isn't this the obvious question?

"Course I do." Rosie laughs. "But you know, I heard a smart woman say once, she said, 'Fear is a force. You can use it like a crutch and let it cripple you, or you can use it like a slingshot and let it make you soar.'" She picks up her ice water and takes a big sip. "And that smart woman was your grandmother."

It feels strange to be getting to know my grandmother only now that she's dead, but still, I swell with pride.

"And she was right," Rosie continues. "I've never felt braver than when I'm staring an alligator in the face."

Rosie downs the rest of her water and wiggles off the stool. "Oh, girls," she says. "If you *do* see an alligator—don't go giving it any roast beef." She smiles and salutes us on her way out.

"All right, you pesky squirrels." Welles slaps the counter. "What'll it be today? Vanilla, chocolate, or—hey, *Ma*, what's the Surprise Me today?"

Rae knocks her knee into mine, and we sneak a silent laugh together.

"Today? Oh, well, today it's—well, I like to call it Full Dinner."

"*Full Dinner?* Come on, Ma! What's in that, anyway?"

"Oh, it's . . . well, let's see. . . ." She gets quiet for a few moments and then says, "I forgot."

Welles sighs. "Okay, squirrels, you name the flavor. My treat."

I dare myself to look that alligator in the face.

"Surprise Me!" I declare.

Welles lowers his eyebrows. "You sure, now?"

On second thought, I order vanilla. Rae orders chocolate.

I guess that when it comes to ice cream, there's really no good reason to take any foolish risks.

The sun's almost down by the time my dad picks us up from the Laundromat. We've had time to fold, refold, and take a few more postables of Rae "surfing" with the rolling basket. My dad apologizes for his lateness but monologues about the refrigerator he's picked out (*IceExpress! Turbocool!*) nearly the whole way home.

As we drive up the curving gravel road toward the house, we can see the twins huddled over something in the yard. Beatrice looks up and starts waving wildly to us, calling out, "You guys! I have proof! I have proof!"

"It's not proof!" Henry shouts.

"Proof of what, Beatrice?" my dad asks as we park and get out of the car.

My mom and Uncle A.J. come out onto the porch to see what all the fuss is about.

"Proof that my kitten is *real*! He left us a gift!"

And that's when I notice the twins are standing over a dead rat.

"Looks like we got ourselves a Free Willy here," my dad says.

"If you ask me, it doesn't take that much to escape from those humane rattraps you guys like," Uncle A.J. says. He hasn't been thrilled with the latest rat-control measure, pre-ferring to go with the "all-out shock and awe," as he calls it—meaning deadly traps and lethal poisons. But he lost in a family vote, six to one.

"But Dad," Beatrice says, "it was injured! You can tell if you look at it."

My dad kneels down and studies it. "Well, Beatrice, you are indeed *right*!" He starts explaining to the rest of us. "If you examine it closely, you can see that the rat's neck has been dislocated, quite possibly from a very recent predatory strike. The fact that the body remains pliable tells us that rigor mortis hasn't set in—"

"*Okay*, thanks, we get it, Dad," I say.

"How do we know it wasn't Barbara?" Henry says. "Igua-nas can also attack rats, can't they, Dad?"

"*Iguanas are herbivores!*" Beatrice shouts.

"Exactly! That would explain why Barbara just left it here! Just because she doesn't eat rats doesn't mean she wouldn't attack one! Does it, Dad?"

"Oh, sure, I guess that could be argued. We don't really know—"

The twins start bickering loudly, and my mom shepherds them inside, since it's starting to get dark. Uncle A.J. brings out a flashlight and a plastic bag, and my dad carefully bags up the corpse.

"Well, one down, about a hundred to go," Uncle A.J. says.

My dad holds out the bag in front of him, one last glimpse before he puts it in the bin. "Well, sorry, little buddy," he says. "Here's to happier trails."

"Yeah, sorry, little rat." Then Rae smiles at us and, in a stage-worthy voice, says, "Let your spirit soar!"

Soar. I think of what Rosie told us at the ice cream counter. *Fear—you can use it like a slingshot and let it make you soar.*

They all start back to the house. Rae turns around and looks at me. "Coming?"

"Yeah, in a minute," I tell her.

She gives me a weird look but turns and bounds up the steps anyway. Which is good, because I don't really want to explain anything right now. I think I might be ready for that slingshot.

Chapter 13

Slingshot

Minutes later, I am walking down the worn path that leads to Mitchell's house. I almost chicken out three times. The first time, it's because of what's in my hand. But at least I come bearing gifts, which is apparently important. The second time, my brain wants to tell me how weird he is. But I remind myself that I've heard people at school whisper the same thing about me, so I power on. The third time, I start to wonder what the symptoms of a heart attack might be, because I might just be having one. And then I remember that fear probably feels a lot like a heart attack, and I breathe deep—three counts in, four out. It actually does help.

And I keep walking. *And* making kissing noises, to be safe.

When I finally reach his house, just as I'm starting to worry that I might have a *fourth* chicken-y event, the door opens. Mitchell's mom steps out, saying, "Okay, kiddo, I'll see you after my shift!"

She turns around and sees me there. I hide my gift behind my back. No need to freak her out.

"Oh, hi again, Edith," she says.

I cringe. She came over to the house the other day, and my mom introduced me. "Actually, you can call me Edie," I say.

She smiles. "Okay, well, hi, Edie. Good to see you again. You here to see Mitchell?"

I smile and nod.

She pokes her head back inside the door. "Mitchell? You've got company."

He comes to the door. "Hey, Edie."

"Don't talk long. You're responsible for Colvin tonight while I'm at work."

"I know, Mom."

She kisses him on the cheek, and he shrugs it off, wiping his cheek on his shoulder, turning pink. I feel his embarrassment.

His mom drives off, and Mitchell looks at me a little uncomfortably. My cheeks feel warm, but before I can even *think* of what to say, there's a clanging sound from the other room.

"Be right back," he says—and when he reappears, he has Colvin slung over his shoulder.

"Hi, Colvin," I say, although I'm pretty much speaking to Colvin's butt.

Mitchell gives me an apologetic smile, then spins around so I can see his little brother's face. Colvin looks annoyed, probably at being taken away from his clanging things.

"Say hi," Mitchell says to Colvin.

"No," Colvin says, his mouth snapping into a tight frown.

"Say hi or I eat your baby toe."

"No!"

Mitchell turns back around to face me. He opens his mouth wide and pretends like he's about to chomp down on Colvin's foot, but then Colvin starts squealing out, *"Hihihihihi!"*

"Hi hi hi hi!" I say back. It seems appropriate.

"Good. Now go get ready for the movie." He plucks Colvin off his shoulder and sets him on the floor.

"Hihihihihihi—"

So this is what normal kids are like. For a second I miss Henry and Beatrice. But it's only a second.

"Hey, Cole, go on, I'll be right there."

But Colvin just stands there. "Fish are friends, not food."

151

"They're what?" I ask.

Colvin's voice gets even louder as he begins to chant, "Fish are friends! Not food! Fish are friends! Not food—"

"It's his favorite line from *Finding Nemo*," Mitchell says over his little brother's voice. "He's only seen it about three hundred times."

Now Colvin's quoting movies too?

"I'll be right back," Mitchell says. He steers Colvin away from the door. I hear him settle him onto the couch. Then he's back. "Okay, eighth time, sorry," he says. "Now—"

With Colvin out from between us, I almost have my fifth chicken-out, but I think about that slingshot again, and I know I need to do this.

"I have something. . . ." I try the droopy-eye-contact thing, but I feel suddenly shy and my eyes spring away from his before even the I'm-listening point. "Something for you."

And then I hand the bag to him.

He holds it up with a confused—maybe even pained?— look on his face. "A . . . a *rat*? Is he— Oh, he's dead."

It suddenly hits me that somehow I've confused flirting with, oh, *bringing a guy a dead rat*. Ugh. A rat is nothing like a Tic Tac!

I try to explain. "I—I . . . *uh* . . . it's for the snakes—"

"No, this is *awesome*."

"You like it?"

"Yeah, Imelda loves rats. I mean, all of them do. Thanks, Edie."

I feel myself smile. *Keep going. Keep trying. Figure out what you have in common.*

Well, it's not snakes. And it's not *The Godfather.*

What about—I think about Petunia's list—stars? Item five, the next item, is "wish upon a shooting star." Everyone likes stars, right? Maybe he'll want to make that wish with me!

"Um, so . . . doyouliketoseestars?" My words come out like a sprung leak.

"Sea stars?" His forehead creases. "Are you asking me something about starfish?"

"No, I mean . . ." I try to breathe and slow down my words. "Do you like to *see* stars?"

"You mean stars in the sky? Do I like *those?*"

"Um, yeah."

"Yeah, I guess I do," he says.

"Yeah, well, me too." Great. Now that we've established that, I have to go through another round of questions—just to see if he'll go out stargazing with me? This is exhausting! And I haven't even made him laugh yet!

My gaze settles on his red shoe laces. *Make him laugh even if you have to give him a sort of hard time.*

"Nice shoelaces," I say. "Where—where'd you, uh, get them?"

"My shoelaces? I don't . . . really *know*?" He says this in a strange way, like he's grasping for some sort of clue. "Why?"

"Well, because . . . um, well . . ." *Santa called and he wants his shoelaces back.* It's so bad I can't even finish the sentence. I start to actually back away.

This is not flirting. This is *alienating*. I feel like I have slingshot myself into a concrete wall. *Splat.*

I can't look at him. I just can't. But I hear him say, "It's kind of cloudy tonight, but you can see a couple."

I glance up. He's gazing at the sky. A few stars break through the murkiness of the night clouds.

"The rest of the week's supposed to be clearer," he says.

Then he looks at me like he has no idea of what a dork I really am, and for a few small seconds, I actually sort of believe it. But—

"Hihihihihihihi."

"I think you're being summoned," I say.

"Hang on. Let me—"

But before he can finish his sentence, Colvin leaps into sight and attaches himself to Mitchell's leg like a barnacle. Mitchell tries to pry his little brother off, and says, "Well, I better, uh, save myself from this scary monster."

Colvin roars loudly.

"Okay, well, see you around?" I ask.

"Yeah, sorry, catch you later. And thanks for the rat!" he calls out as the screen door shuts.

"Byebyebyebye." Colvin's voice grows fainter as he pulls his brother down the hall.

I'm not really sure what just happened, and I wish I could talk to Rae about it. But when I get back to our room, she's kicked back on her bed, chatting breezily on the phone, and it feels like we're worlds apart. Boys and friends and flirting all seem to come so naturally to her.

She notices me and tilts her chin a little in a greeting. She holds up two fingers and mouths, excitedly, "Two bars!" I give her a thumbs-up.

"Edie's back," she says into her phone. "So I better go."

Pause.

"Yeah, me too."

But she doesn't hang up. Instead, she giggles and hides a smile.

"No, *you* say it."

Eyes flash to me, then back down again. Head folds forward, hand over receiver. Muffled voice. A giggle.

Longer pause.

Let her talk. I'd be talking on the phone if I could too—to Taylor. But visiting day is still a full week and a half away!

Maybe I should just write to Taylor at camp. At least I'll have *some* adventures to report.

I pull out a notepad from my couch-side table and start writing.

> *Hey Taylor, I'm having such a fun and exciting summer. Guess what? I gave a boy a dead rat!*

Wait. Not that.

I rip off the sheet and start again. At least I can write to her about the Hurricane.

"Crap, I lost him!" Rae says, glaring at her phone. "Yep, back to zero bars again. Why am I not surprised?" Then she glances at me. "Sorry. That was Leo."

"Yeah, I kind of guessed," I say, but I smile.

"So, where'd you go?" Rae asks.

"Oh, well . . . over to Mitchell's."

Her eyes get big. "Did you flirt with him?"

"Uh, no. Not really. Not successfully, at least."

She laughs. Then she notices the piece of paper.

"What's that? Are you writing a letter?"

"Oh. Yeah."

"I told you, you can call Klaus anytime you want." She wiggles the phone.

"No, this is to a friend. My friend Taylor."

"Oh. Well, you know you can still use my phone if you want to call her too, right?"

"Thanks. I would, but she's at camp, and . . ." I look at Rae. She does seem to be listening. "She's with another friend. And it's sort of, well, driving me a little crazy."

To say the least.

"Well, I totally understand how you feel, cuz."

"You do?"

"*Hello?* Who's not at Shakespeare camp this summer with her boyfriend and her besties?" she says. "That would be yours truly."

I give her a smile. Could she really understand how I feel?

"So what's your letter say?"

"Oh, well, it's—" I look down at it.

Guess what? I snuck out at night! I broke into an abandoned building! The police were called!

But as I read it over, I realize I sound less like a spirited adventurer and more like a pathetic juvenile delinquent. Do I really expect Taylor to be impressed by *this*?

"Nothing really," I say, shrugging—hoping to disguise my disappointment as nonchalance. I tear off the sheet, crumple it up, and put the tablet away.

Chapter 14

Carp-y Diem

It's the Fourth of July. While the rest of the country is celebrating, Pinne, Florida, just gives the holiday a droopy-eyed nod. No fireworks, no parades, no bands playing the national anthem. At Beatrice's urging, we've dressed in our brightest shades of red, white, and blue, and we're all wearing glow-in-the-dark necklaces that my dad bought for us at Augustus Tools.

So, it's pretty much like any other day, just a little more blinding.

Dani's taped a few streamers to the ceiling of the diner, but the humidity has made most of them fall, and they drape listlessly over the mostly empty tables. One dangles into the sugar basket of a four-top.

"So how's the hunt for the Batman whompus thing going?" Uncle A.J. asks my dad and the twins as we slide into our usual table.

As Dani sets up our table, my dad starts droning on about how they've started a search for the sparrow-tailed kite, since Bachman's warbler has proved too elusive. That's when the door opens, ushering in a gust of warm air—and Mitchell.

My dad speaks first. "Well, howdy there, Mitchell. What brings you to the B-Ditty?" It's how he now refers to the BEST Diner in Town, with no regard for the cruel and unusual embarrassment he causes me.

"*Mitchell!*" my mom says, clasping her hands to her chest. "I'm so sorry. I completely forgot!"

Mitchell's smile turns awkward. "It *was* tonight? My mom said you'd invited me—"

"Yes, yes! Of course. We're thrilled you're here! Kids, everyone, let's make room for Mitchell."

"Sit here!" Beatrice says, moving over a seat so that Mitchell can sit between her and Henry.

Though I'm secretly excited to see him, I'm also incredibly nervous. For one, I'm not exactly sure what transpired between us the other evening—dead rats and *sea stars*, really? And for two, there's my freak show of family, decked out in glowing necklaces and patriotic colors . . . and that's even before they open their mouths. If *I* haven't scared him off yet, they will undoubtedly do just that tonight.

I send a worried glance over at Rae, but she's grinning at Mitchell. Then she says in her raspy *Godfather* voice, "It's an offer you can't refuse."

And the two of them laugh together again, while I can only spectate and paste on a smile. His eyes meet mine for a fleeting second, but I look away and end up studying the blue plaid of the tablecloth. So much for eye contact.

Dani comes over to take our orders. Everyone goes for burgers (and fried pickles) again, but not me. I decide to try something unexpected—unpredictable! adventurous!—and order an omelet.

The second Dani brings our drinks, Beatrice launches in on Mitchell. "Guess what human fingernails have in common with a snake's scales?"

Mitchell looks perplexed. "Um . . ."

Henry answers. "They're both a form of skin."

"*Errrrrr!*" Beatrice says. "Both human fingernails and a snake's scales are made up of keratin."

"That's basically what I was saying!" Henry argues. Then *he* turns to Mitchell. "Do you know the definition of *ecdysis*?"

Before Mitchell can even try to answer, Beatrice blurts it out. "It's when a snake sheds its skin! Oh! You should know this, Mitchell, since you like snakes. It's spelled E-C—"

"Beatrice!" I scold.

"D-Y-S-I-S."

Mitchell just smiles at her. "Cool."

Dealing with my own bad social skills is hard enough—now I have to deal with the twins'! I need Rae, but her attention is now on her phone. I even try to snag my mom's attention, but the adults are too wrapped up in discussing the details of the housework to pay attention.

"That roof probably needs to be redone," Uncle A.J. is saying.

"Oh, A.J." My mom sighs. "Can't we just repair those shingles where it's leaking?"

"And by 'we,' you mean me," A.J. scoffs.

"We also need to decide on paint colors," my dad says. "Now, me, I'm partial to Summer Shadow for the exterior of the house."

Henry continues the siege on Mitchell. "If an alligator ate you, do you know how long it would take until he completely digested you?"

"I . . . have no idea," Mitchell says. "A week?"

"It could take a hundred days!" Henry says.

"Maximum," Beatrice argues.

I take a breath. If Rae won't save Mitchell, it's up to me. "Speaking of alligators, we met a—"

But Henry keeps on. "And did you know that if a snake

is born with two heads, the two heads will fight each other for food?"

"That's pretty incredible," Mitchell says. He looks across the table to me. "What about alligators?"

"We met an alligator trapper the other day," I tell him. "And she said there was a report—"

"Where did you meet an alligator trapper?" Beatrice asks.

"Wait. A gator sighting?" Mitchell sits straight. "Where exactly? Did she say?"

"Over by some store? A Buy 'n' Tote, I think? But it sounded like a false report. She said they've been getting a lot of those. The alligator was gone when she got there."

Mitchell looks extremely interested, but Beatrice won't let up. "Edith, *where* did you meet an alligator trapper?"

"At the—" And then I remember I wasn't supposed to be at the ice cream/hardware store on laundry day. That's all I need is Beatrice tattling. I press my knee into Rae's. *Help.* But I've lost her to her phone. I try to distract the twins. "Didn't you guys bring your Samurai Sudoku?"

It doesn't work.

"Oh, Mitchell!" Henry says. "There's this African snake, and it swallows eggs whole. And then, inside the snake's body, there are spikes that crack the egg open, so the yolk and stuff can be digested. And then, afterward, the snake vomits up a little shell package!"

"*Henry*, gross. We're about to eat," I say. Just then Dani brings the plates. I look down at my omelet. Bad choice.

"Oh, Edith!" Beatrice eyes my plate. "I wonder how many African snakes—"

"I think we *should* change the subject." I realize I sound a little like my mom, but I'm getting pretty desperate.

"Okay." Beatrice turns back to Mitchell. "Did you know we have a kitten?"

"You have a kitten?" Mitchell asks.

"No," Henry says. He starts explaining to Mitchell how there's no proof, and Beatrice tells him there is *because Henry saw the droppings himself.*

"It's called scat," Henry says.

"What is?" Beatrice says.

"The droppings." Henry looks smug. "The scientific name is scat."

My face is on fire. My stomach is in knots. I need Rae to save this dinner—seize it, carpe it, take it hostage, whatever it takes, but she's still preoccupied with her phone. I nudge her frantically with my knee under the table. "Rae, *help*!" I whisper. "Mayday, mayday! Emergency!"

"Can you believe this, Edie? Yay for dirty laundry! We're up to two hundred and forty-two likes on Instagram!"

I'm at my breaking point. I need to escape. I get up from the table.

"Edith? Where are you going?" my mom asks.

"Bathroom," I murmur.

"Wrap the seat!" she calls out after me.

I walk faster, but still I can't get away quickly enough.

In the bathroom, I snap off my glow necklace and pat down my overheated face. I look at myself in the mirror and notice a smudge of dirt over my left eyebrow, probably a remnant of today's indentured servitude—a day full of fetching tools for my mom and uncle and carrying boxes down from the attic. I feel an extra flutter of annoyance at Rae for not mentioning the smudge to me.

I lean in a little closer, studying my own eyes, looking for that stormy gray that Petunia and I supposedly share. What color is "stormy," anyway? I hope for something dramatic—a bright-gold fleck or two, like a flash of lightning. But right now, all I see in my eyes is the color of an ordinary overcast day.

The door swings open and Dani walks in, untying her apron. "Oh, hi, Edie." She washes her hands under the faucet and gives me a slightly concerned look in the mirror. "How are you doing?"

"Okay, I guess."

"You don't seem okay."

"Oh." I say. It's a little awkward. For the first time, I wish for a movie quote, or Shakespeare, to save me from having to really answer.

"It's okay. Of course you miss her."

"Petunia?" I ask.

"Who else? I know you never got to meet her, but she's part of you anyway," Dani says. She makes it sound so simple, and maybe it is. "You know, I miss her too. Maybe not that snake of hers that she kept wrapped around her shoulders, though."

"Herbie?" I smile. I might even be starting to feel a little affection for him.

"Yeah, well . . ." She turns to face me, leaning into the sink, putting one hand on her hip. "I never believed he was a service snake."

"A service snake?" I ask.

"You know those service animals that people use—people with seizures and diabetes, and that kind of thing? Usually they use dogs, but Petunia said that Herbie was a service snake. Snake therapy, she called it. Always wanted to say to her, *yeah*, maybe that thing is making *you* feel better, but it sure as heck is scaring the tiddledywinks out of the rest of us!" She laughs. "Honestly, snake therapy! I mean, you ever hear of such a thing?"

"Well . . . uh, no," I say.

Dani chuckles. "She could be a real rascal at times, that

Petunia." She inspects her smile in the mirror and tucks a strand of hair behind her ear. "All right, well, I'll see you back at your table. We've got some great desserts tonight."

"Right," I say, but I'm not quite ready to return to the disaster of a conversation that I escaped.

I think about what Dani told me. I wonder what snake therapy is, and if I might need some of that after this summer is over.

When I finally return to the table, there are platefuls of chocolate cake and big bowls of banana pudding waiting. We'll *never* get out of here.

"How many times does a hummingbird's heart beat per minute?" Henry is asking. "Dad, Mom, you're not allowed to answer."

"Two hundred?" Rae guesses.

"I'll go two fifty," Uncle A.J. says.

"Five hundred?" Mitchell says. "I know it's super fast."

"Edith?" Henry asks.

"I'm not playing," I say.

"Well, you're all wrong! It can beat up to one thousand two hundred and sixty times."

"I've got one," my dad says, smiling mischievously. "How much wood would a woodchuck chuck, if a woodchuck could chuck wood?"

I shovel some more chocolate cake into my face. Might as well enjoy *something*.

"*Daaaad,*" Henry whines. "That's a tongue twister. It's not a real question!"

"No, Henry, it *is* a real question, and I know this!" Beatrice says. "Seven hundred and eleven pounds of wood a day! Right, Dad?"

"Well, theoretically, of course," my dad says, and he and Beatrice laugh and laugh.

I shovel faster.

On the way out, my mom offers to give Mitchell a ride home with us.

"Thanks, but I rode my bike," he says.

"But it's dark. I don't think it's safe—"

"It's okay, Mrs. Posey."

But, not surprisingly, it turns outs my mom's offer isn't technically an *offer* but a polite demand. She has Uncle A.J. attach Mitchell's bike to the back of the van, and we all cram in for the ride home. Mitchell squeezes in next to me, and my heart squeezes up a little when he does.

"So," he says to me in a hushed voice, "about those stars . . ."

I glance over at him.

"You know." The side of his cheek reveals his glorious cheek dent. "*Sea stars.*"

"Oh, *right!*" I say.

Rae looks over at us.

"So it's supposed to stay really clear out tonight. You guys want to go see some stars up on Stone Hill?" Even though he's addressing both Rae and me, his voice is still soft and quiet, and *very* close to my ear.

"Yes," I say.

"Wait. What?" Rae says.

I give her a tight-smiling, wide-eyed look that translates into "I'll tell you about it as soon as I can."

"Okay," Mitchell whispers. "See you guys up there—about nine?"

"Sounds great," I say, even though I'm suddenly terrified. Wait, no, exhilarated. No, terrified. Well, I don't know exactly how I feel, but I do know that my heart is fluttering as fast as a hummingbird's. One thousand two hundred and sixty beats a minute sounds about right.

Chapter 15

Sky High

"Okay, I don't get it," Rae says. We're sitting on one of Petunia's old blankets, staring up at the planetarium-bright sky. "The Big Dipper just looks like a box." She swats at a mosquito.

"Yeah, sort of," I say. "Can you see the Summer Triangle?" I try to point out three bright stars, but she shakes her head.

"They all look the same. Ouch!" She slaps her ankle. "These bugs are killing me."

I sigh. She doesn't seem to appreciate all that went into us getting here. I knew my dad felt bad about us having the lamest Fourth of July celebration ever. So, with my mom having headed straight to bed after the diner, I convinced my dad that after three busy days of working, Rae and I deserved a glimpse of nature's own fireworks display. A study of the stars and constellations.

So he gave us permission. He even told me he was proud of my gumption.

"I know, the bugs are bad," I say. "But just look up again. See those three stars?"

She squints up at the stars. "Edie, I don't see anything other than the Big Dipper. That's the only one I know."

I try to be encouraging. "See? You know *something*."

She waves her hands around her head, trying to clear the mosquitoes away. "Everyone knows the Big Dipper. Big deal."

"You can probably see Ursa Minor too. The Little Dipper. The North Star is at the end of its handle. Right there."

She sighs. "I don't see it. Where's Mitchell, anyway? He's late."

"Only about five minutes," I say.

"Okay, but I'm getting about a hundred bites a minute, so he's about five hundred mosquito bites too late." She scratches her arm. "I think we should go."

"Not yet," I say. "Please?"

"Edie, it's not like I got a say in this."

"I thought you'd be excited. It's all about seizing the day, right? Or, okay, the night?" I say. Truthfully, I was always a little worried about her enthusiasm about item five on the list. "Wish upon a shooting star" is one of those things that sounds good in theory but happens to involve a lot of sitting and waiting and staring and waiting some more.

"All you told me was that you failed flirting with him. You didn't say you asked him out!"

I suck in a breath. "I didn't ask him out. I just asked him if he liked stars, since it's on the list."

"What's the big deal with the list anyway? I know it was kind of fun in the beginning, but now, it's like—well, why? I can think of a million more postable things."

We can't give up now! But if I tell her why the list means so much to me, she'll know how boring and no fun I really am. So I just blurt out, "It's for Petunia."

She turns to me.

I continue. "I, uh, never got to meet her, like you did. So it's—well, kind of like getting to know her. Just doing the things she did." And when I say it, it actually doesn't feel that untrue.

"*Oh*," she says, like she understands. "Okay, I get it. But, Edie, the stars actually come out every night, so—"

"Well, sure, but . . . just look up. It's superclear out tonight, and we're here now, and it's pretty amazing." And it is. The sky is vast. The stars are brilliant.

"I know, but *now* is making me feel like an all-you-can-eat buffet for these mosquitoes."

"Just a little longer, please." *Maybe Mitchell will show up.* "Maybe we'll see a shooting star."

"Or we actually *could* catch malaria. Wonder which is more likely."

"The shooting star," I joke. I recite a statistic that I just made up but I'm sure is factual. "More people see shooting stars than catch malaria." At some point, I seem to have turned into Henry.

She sighs. "Okay, five more minutes, but if nothing happens, I'm going."

We wait, staring up at the sky, swatting the air, smacking our necks, our exposed arms, our feet.

The sky is sparkly, but it remains still.

"Edie, this kind of bites. *Literally.*"

"Well, you can't leave without making a wish," I say, trying to buy time. *Where is he?* "Just pick out *one* star to wish on—even an ordinary one."

She looks up at the sky again and takes a big breath. And starts coughing, gagging. "I think I swallowed a bug!" She starts to retch.

I hand her my water. She gargles, forcefully spits it all out, and wipes her mouth with the back of her hand.

"I can't deal with these bugs. I'm leaving."

"Now?"

"Now."

"What about your wish?"

"I *wish* that I could leave. And I'm going to make that come true." She stands up. "You coming?"

I don't know what scares me most. Being alone up here in the dark, or being around a boy who may actually like me. I decide to take my chances.

"I'll be home soon," I say, but she just turns and walks away.

I sit and stare out into the darkness. I try not to think about what lurks around me. I try not to think about the fact that I'm alone in a strange place at night. And I try not to think about how weird it is to sit here making kissing noises. To scare off the snakes. I mean, just in case.

I've made three wishes on three separate stars. To be daring and adventurous, like Rae—like Petunia. To have my best friend back. And on the third one, I wish—

I see a flashlight bouncing around in the darkness, as if floating clumsily along by itself. I wonder if it's Rae coming back for me, but I don't hear the pink flip-floppiness of her feet. This is more of a trudge.

"Mitchell?" I call out.

"Sorry I'm late," he says, close enough now where I can see him.

That last one must have been a lucky star.

He sits next to me and flips down the hood of his sweat-shirt. We look in each other's directions but, thankfully, it's too dark for eye contact.

He holds out a small clay pot. Inside is a lemony-smelling candle. "Citronella. It's supposed to keep the mosquitoes away."

"How'd you know they were going to be so bad?"

"I've sort of lived in Florida all my life," he says. "You get to know a lot about bugs."

Then he pulls out a book of matches. I realize I wouldn't know how to light a match—I've been taught to stay away from them. I watch him take a quick strike. A flame appears, and he sets it to the wick.

"That's so amazing," I say, and I mean it.

He laughs like I've made a joke. At least I've made him laugh without making fun of his shoelaces.

I take a big whiff of the lemony air and smile. Despite the fact that Rae's already left, despite the fact that there are probably snakes around, despite the fact that it's late and I'm still out—despite all the should-nots going on right now, I'm feeling pretty good. Until he asks, "Where's Rae?"

Of course.

"Oh," I say. "She went home. The bugs were driving her crazy and—well, she wasn't having fun."

I wonder if he's going to politely excuse himself and leave, but he doesn't. He just asks if I like Slim Jims.

"Slim Jims?" I ask. A forbidden food. Seen but never consumed.

"You never had one?"

"No. Never."

"Want to try it?"

"I don't know. What's it taste like?" I always imagined them a little like turkey jerky, which is something I tried on a group dare at recess. Actually, it would have been more daring *not* to—to be the one who didn't buckle to the pressure, but I buckled. It tasted more like fish than turkey, and the flavor was so unpleasant and strong that I still remember it. A lasting scar of peer pressure, I guess.

"It's kinda like pepperoni," he says.

He unwraps the little stick and hands it to me. I take the first bite—a little nibble. It's chewy and a bit spicy. It qualifies as junk food. It's probably horrible for me. But it doesn't taste as bad as I would have thought.

"It does taste like pepperoni," I say, smiling a little. I give it back to him and he bites right into it, like I have no germs at all. Oddly, I feel flattered. It's like the opposite of having cooties.

I glance at him from the corner of my eye. He's staring up at the sky.

"You know the constellations?" he asks.

"Some of them."

"When I look up there, I just see a billion questions."

"Like what?" I ask. Because I feel like I want to answer them *all*.

"Like, what's going on out there? Is it really just rocks and fire and gas and stuff?"

"Or is there something out there like us? Looking back at us?"

"Exactly," he says. "And, like, how many stars are we looking at?"

"Oh. Actually, I know the answer. It's about two thousand."

"Where did you learn that?" he asks.

"From the twins." As soon as I say it, I realize I kind of miss them. Just a little. I'm sure a few extra seconds alone with them would cure me of that, but still. "They can be annoying, *but*."

"Yeah, I know how that is," he says. "You met my little brother. The one who wouldn't shut up."

"Yeah, he *is* a talker," I say. "I guess the twins are too—they just have more words to choose from. Maybe we all were like that when we were younger."

"Not me," he says.

I give him a yeah-right look. "You probably just don't remember."

He hesitates. "I remember. I actually went three years without talking."

I wonder if he's joking, but in the glow of the candle, I see only the hint of a smile on his face.

"You mean, really?" I ask.

"Yep. Not a word. From when I was about five till I was about eight."

"How—" I'm not sure if it's a rude question or not, but I ask it anyway. "How come?"

He tilts his head and smiles a little. "I don't know. Maybe because I could only count to five and my favorite word was *poo*. Wasn't that impressive."

I laugh. Okay, it starts as a laugh, but then it threatens to mutate into one of those awful, uncontrollable, weird nervous laugh-snort-chortle fits, so I hold my breath and bury my face in my knees, trying to smother it out.

"You okay?"

"Yeah," I say, as soon as I'm sure I can talk. I feel like I owe him some sort of explanation. But what am I going to say? "So, I have this nervous condition. Especially around boys I might secretly like." I think not!

Thankfully, he seems to be pretty interested in staring into the night sky, and not too weirded out by me. I wait until the urge to laugh passes, then ask, "So do you recognize any constellations?"

"Nah, I just kind of look at everything."

I gaze up and try to see what he sees. Not Orion the

Hunter, or Cassiopeia the Queen, but just the overall brilliance of the sky.

A breeze blows past us, and I breathe it in to calm myself. It gives me a shiver, and I rub my arms briskly.

Mitchell pulls off his sweatshirt and hands it over to me. "Here," he says. "Put this on."

I hesitate. "You don't want it?"

"Nah, I'm fine," he says.

"Thanks," I say, and slip the sweatshirt on. It feels warm underneath, like a good hug, and I try to hide the secret thrill I feel. I pull the sleeves over my hands and tuck my head into the hood, and I lie back on the blanket to get a better look at the stars. He does too.

"You ever been on the Gravitron?" he asks me.

"What's a *Gravitron*?"

"You know, that thing at carnivals and stuff—it's a ride. It's this thing you get in and it spins around so fast, you just stick to the wall."

It sounds like science. The true effect of centrifugal force. "What's it like?"

"It's kind of like this," he says. "It's like the Earth is giant Gravitron."

I close my eyes and try to feel it, and after a few minutes, I do—the strong force of gravity pressing me into the spinning

Earth. Like I couldn't move if even I wanted to. And I really, truly don't want to.

I hear him breathing. I wonder if he can hear my heart beating.

"See what I mean?" he asks.

"Yeah," I say. Maybe I can convince my father to take me next time the carnival comes to town. And maybe I'll actually be brave enough to get on the ride. "It sounds like a fun ride."

"Yeah. It is. As long as you don't step in a puked-up corn dog afterward. There's always someone who loses it when the ride stops."

Snort. It starts, but I don't dare allow myself to laugh again. Not a chance.

Then he asks, "How many miles do you think we're actually looking at?"

"Oh," I say. "I know that too. Nineteen quadrillion."

"Nineteen *quadrillion*? That's a *lot*."

"Yeah," I say, and try not to think about the fact that with all those quadrillions of miles around, there's only a me eighteen inches between the two of us.

And then we both just smile up at the stars in silence. I'm battling to keep my eyes open, because I'm far from ready for this ride to stop.

Chapter 16

Fall

I am falling off the bottom of the Earth. Falling in this slow-motion way—a little floaty fall. I am nearing a star, somewhere outside Earth's atmosphere—the star doesn't look like it's twinkling anymore, it's just burning, burning away. I'm feeling hot. Then *hotter*. Then I am speeding toward the fiery star, the float having disappeared from the fall. I'm being pulled now, faster, and *faster*, and—

I try to scream. It feels funny in my throat, as though it's being pulled out of my lungs. I gag, cough, I can't breathe—

"Hey, Edie."

I sit up. Open my eyes. I am on the blanket. Sitting next to Mitchell. Wearing a gray sweatshirt. *His* sweatshirt. In the already bright and broiling morning sun.

"You okay?" He has this look on his face, like he's amused but isn't sure he should be.

"I was having a bad dream. I couldn't breathe." My throat feels like someone just cleaned it out with a metal brush. Which means I've been snoring. I've probably snored and snorted all night, and I am *mortified.* "I'm sorry."

"No, *I'm* sorry. I kept you out all night."

Oh, no. Snoring and maybe even drooling are suddenly the least of my concerns. I jump up, like I've just been given a shot of adrenaline. I'm going to be in trouble all over again.

"I better go," I say, sort of frantically.

"Okay," he says, very *un*frantically. "Let's go, then."

I want to tell him I had a good time. No, a great time. No, even better—a *stellar* time, *hardy har har*—but I feel suddenly shy on the fast walk back to our houses. I think about the possible creatures in the grass, but there's no way I'm making kissing sounds. *No way.* I'll just have to take my chances.

Right where the paths between our houses split, we stop and look at each other. Or we try to, but our eyes dart around.

"Well, it was . . . fun."

"Yeah." He smiles. I notice his wild hair looks even *wilder* in the morning, but it doesn't look so strange to me anymore. "Hey, how far did you say we could see? You know, when you're looking at stars?"

"Oh. About nineteen quadrillion miles," I say.

"Wow. That's pretty awesome."

"I mean, not every night, but on a good night."

"Yeah, so . . ." That dimple of his makes a welcome reappearance. "It was kind of a good night."

I feel my face catch on fire. I feel a laugh bubbling up inside my snore-torn throat. It *was* a good night. But I can't say it back. Not that I don't want to—it's just that I *physically* can't. I'm laughing too hard. Snortling and snickering and chortling and making all those awful kinds of laugh noises that I fought so hard to silence last night.

After a few eternities, I manage some sort of apology. "Sorry, I, uh . . ."

"Yeah, okay," he says. "Guess I'll catch you later."

"Yeah," I say, trying very hard to match his casual tone, despite the feeling that I've messed up this good-bye pretty epically. And I'm not sure he will catch me later, because it's very possible that I could be grounded, not just for the summer, but for the rest of my life.

I picture the calamity that awaits me at the house. Have the police been called? Is my mom a sobbing mess? Has my dad summoned a search party? And what about Rae? What's she told them?

As I near the house, I hear the raised voices of my mom

182

and Uncle A.J. I can only catch a few words—"horrible," "can't believe," "your fault." Things are pretty intense. But maybe this time, I should go in there, standing tall and unashamed. I'll tell them all to calm down—everything's okay. I didn't mean to stay out all night, but I'm safe.

My mom will pull me into a massive hug, just grateful to have me home. She'll say, "I'm just glad to have you home, Edie!" She'll call me Edie.

My dad will kiss me on the forehead and tell me he was lost without me, his smart girl. His unsung genius.

The twins will ask me how I did it—how I managed to survive all the dangers. For once, they'll want to learn something from *me*. "What's it like to be brave?" they'll ask. "Can you show us how?"

Uncle A.J. will give me my own nickname, like Boss or Champ or Sparkplug. Or Firecracker. I really like Firecracker.

And *Rae*. Rae, of course, will be full of admiration. She'll call me the adventurer. The carpe noctemer. The stay-out-all-nighter. Edie the Gutsy One. The Courageous One. Or at least, the One Who Was Not Felled by Mosquitoes.

But when I walk in the door, no one seems to notice. The grown-ups *are* shouting at each other, sure, but it's not about me.

It's about a broken toilet.

"The pipes are ancient—what do you expect?" It's Uncle A.J.

"I expect you to fix it, that's what!" my mom shouts.

"Welles doesn't sell toilets—and he doesn't have the right parts. Now, if you're in the market for a Kleenex Kozee—"

"Oh, for the love of *meat loaf*, A.J.! Just drive into Bartow. No reason to stay in this pea-sized town. And anyway, the toilet can be put back together. All you really need to do is repair the floor."

"All I really need to do . . ." Uncle A.J. seethes. "Hannah, if you know so much, why don't you fix it yourself?"

"Maybe we should think about buying a new one," my dad says. "Maybe with one of those Whisper Quiet toilet seats."

But my mom ignores him and turns back to my uncle. "*Fix it myself?* I just may have to! I can probably figure it out faster than you're willing to get off your lazy hindquarters to get it done!"

"Lazy?" Uncle A.J. says. "I'll show you lazy."

My dad continues, "In bone, or maybe a glacier white. I think bisque is kind of outdated."

My mom suddenly sees me standing in the entrance to the kitchen. "Oh, hi, honey. You were up early, huh?"

"Hey there, sugarplum," my dad says. "*Whaaaat's* cracka-lackin'?"

"Not . . . much?" I say, but I feel like a human question

mark. Is this a trick question?

"The crapper's shot," Uncle A.J. says.

It's not really the weeping, relieved welcome I'd expected. My mom and Uncle A.J. go back to their bickering. My dad starts touting the virtues of the Econoflush. I go to look for Rae.

I find her upstairs, still in bed, her back to the door.

"Rae," I whisper.

She doesn't move. I wonder if she's still annoyed with me.

"Rae."

She stirs. *"What?"*

"How can you sleep with all that arguing going on?"

"Who said I was asleep?"

I don't answer. She rolls over and looks at me.

"You *just* got home?"

Where's that look of admiration?

"Yeah, uh—"

"I didn't know you were going to stay up there all night!"

"Me neither, but thanks for covering for me," I say. "Sorry about that."

She blows out a breath, a little disarmed. "You're wearing his sweatshirt."

"Yeah." I take it off. It's getting too hot for it anyway. "I forgot about it, I guess."

"Well, so, did you wish upon a shooting star?" She says this with an edge to her voice.

I make a little laugh breath. "*Nooo*. We didn't see any shooting stars."

"So, what did you do all night?"

I want to tell her everything, but I recognize the look on her face. The look of being left out. I know that feeling way too well. All the freedom and fearlessness of last night starts to quickly fade. "It was . . . *fine*. We just ate Slim Jims and talked a little, and I guess we fell asleep. You should have stayed, though. He brought a candle that kept the bugs away—well, mostly."

But the look on her face doesn't change, and I just want to make everything okay between us.

"He's kind of a space case sometimes, though, you know?" I feel a little jerky saying it, but that vanishes when I see her start to smile.

"I know, right?" And then she laughs, and I seem to be forgiven.

For a few seconds, it feels pretty good. Then I start to feel like total carp for saying something mean about him, especially just for a laugh. "Just kidding," I say. "I just mean, it would have been more fun if you were there."

But she says, "Yeah, he's nice and all, but sometimes he's such an Olaf. You know, the snowman from *Frozen*?"

"Oh, yeah."

And she launches into a scene from the movie, with a dopey-sounding voice. "My name is Olaf, and I like warm hugs!"

She looks at me like she's expecting a laugh, and I deliver. In fact, my laugh feels almost too big for the situation.

She smiles, as if she's pleased to be entertaining me, but that's not really why I'm laughing. It's more a silly, giddy relief of having the dynamic duo back.

Chapter 17

Wish in One Hand

The four of us are out in the shed today—Rae and me, Beatrice and Henry. Over the last few days, our parents have sent us out here several times. They say they want us to sort through things and start to clear everything out, but Rae and I secretly believe it's to keep us out of their hair so they can fight more freely among themselves.

Rae's handing me boxes from the shelves, and I'm sorting through the rusty tools, bags of unplanted seeds, spare lightbulbs, and other collections of not-so-useful things. The twins are supposed to be helping, but instead they're quizzing us. It's like a bad game show, with Rae and me as the reluctant contestants.

"Okay, true or false," Beatrice asks. "Only female crickets can chirp."

"I don't know. True?" I guess.

The twins look at each other and laugh in a nasally, self-righteous way. "*False*, Edith! You didn't know that?"

"Obviously not," I say. "Anyway, when are you guys going to go look for that swallow-tailed kite?"

"*Sparrow*-tailed kite, Edith," Beatrice says. "We couldn't find that bird either. Now we're looking for the Florida scrub jay. It's also endangered."

"Okay, well? I don't think you're going to find a Florida scrub jay in *here*."

"Dad's taking us out later," Beatrice says.

"How about your kitten? Don't you want to check on him?" Rae asks.

"Aristotle? Oh. He only comes out at night."

"She's still the only one who's ever seen it," Henry says.

"I can't help it if he only likes *me*." Beatrice shrugs. "Okay, Rae! This is for you. How many noses does a slug have?"

Rae smiles. "Henry, Beatrice, look this way so I can count."

"She said *slug*," Henry sort of sighs.

"Yeah, and the answer is zero," Beatrice says. "They smell through tentacles! Okay, Edith! How fast can a dragonfly fly?"

"A hundred miles an hour," I say. I'm only partially aware

that Rae is trying to hand something to me—something large, as big as a serving platter.

"You're not even trying!" Beatrice whines.

"Okay, then three miles an hour." I give Beatrice a weary look as I take the big platter thing from Rae.

"Edith!" Beatrice says in a shocked and bewildered tone.

"Beatrice, I don't know then. Fifteen miles an hour? That's my best guess."

But Beatrice doesn't answer. Her eyes are fixed on whatever is in my hands.

I turn to look, and see that I'm holding a wooden plaque. And attached to that plaque is the stiff, stuffed, serpentine body that used to be on the wall in the house. My heart pounds fast in my chest, my neck, my ears. My hands are starting to quiver. My mouth opens as if to scream.

But then I remember everyone is watching me, including my fearless cousin. I make myself smile, and I smile *hard*. And I say, "It's so nice to see you again, Herbie."

The twins have been called away by my dad for another bird-filming field trip, after an enthusiastic exchange about Herbie and his snakishness. ("How can you tell if a snake is about to shed its skin?" "Its eyes look milky." And another. "True or false: rat snakes are also called bean snakes." Annoying buzzing sound. "False! They're called corn snakes!") And

I'm basking in the fact that I held a snake in my hands. Okay, well, not really—I was handed a piece of wood that a dead snake was attached to. But still, I didn't scream, or die, or otherwise lose consciousness. It's not exactly a Taylor-worthy checkmark on Petunia's list of good ideas, but it's the closest I've ever come to *literally handling* one of my biggest fears.

I wish I could share the importance of this moment with Rae. She seems to sense me looking at her as she bags up another round of donations. "Congratulations," she says.

"On what?" I ask.

"On almost touching a dead snake, Edie. I know you're scared of them. It doesn't take a genius to figure it out."

"Oh." I let out a one-syllable laugh. "I guess I *am* obvious, then."

"Yeah, you can be. I don't know why you couldn't have said something to me, though, instead of pretending all this time."

"Well, sorry. It's just embarrassing."

"Don't apologize, Edie." She puts on her melodrama face—eyebrows knitting together, chin lifting—and says, in a flowery voice, "Love means never having to say you're sorry. *Love Story.* Now that's a classic. You *have* to see it sometime."

But for a second, I start to feel a little annoyed. "Rae, if you knew that I—well, that I have a real problem with snakes—then why did you hand Herbie to me?"

She lets her hands drop to her sides. "I wasn't trying to scare you, Edie. I was trying to let you see that you didn't need to be scared. It's like stage fright. The only cure for it is getting up on stage. If you don't do that, you're just stuck with it."

"Oh." It's actually a good point. And it did help a little.

"You know, I don't always understand you."

I sigh. "I know. I shouldn't be scared of snakes. More people die from bee stings than snakebites, I get all that. It's just that when I was little, my dad took me to the zoo—"

I start to tell her the story, but she's turned away again. She's back to sorting the shelves like she's getting paid to do it.

I trail off. She doesn't urge me on. She wanted an explanation, didn't she? But I don't get a chance to ask her why she lost interest because *ding!* She picks up her phone and gasps, "*Oh my god!* I have five bars!"

Of chocolate? Of gold? Oh, five bars of *cell service*, I realize, feeling like I'm finally in the correct century.

"I can't believe it." Only then does she look back at me. "You know what? I'm going to try to FaceTime Leo since I finally can."

It's not like she's asking my permission, but still, I say, "Okay. Go ahead."

"Leo? Leo?" Her voice fades as she steps outside.

"Leo, *Leo, Leo*! O, Leo! Wherefore art thou Leo?" I say to myself, and sigh. Seems like I'm always losing her to the gorgeous and talented Leo. And she's always trying to pass me off on Klaus, the Eeyore of boyfriends.

Through the open door, I can see Mitchell's small house. Things have been a little strange with him since that starry night five days ago. I've seen him around—out in the yard, dealing with the snakes—but we've hardly said more than hi to each other. I guess he's nervous all over again. I can't blame him. I am too. It's weird that sometimes the more you like someone, the harder it is to talk to them.

But I do want to talk to him.

And—hey, don't I have a sweatshirt to return? Something to give him helps, like Rae said.

I run into the house and up the stairs. I grab the sweatshirt from our room. When I step back into the hall, my nerves start to tingle. I make myself keep moving—out the back door, down the steps. Even though it no longer feels like completely forbidden territory to me, I'm still a little jittery walking through the yard. I try not to look in the direction of the enclosure, but out of the corner of my eye I see something move, and I jump.

It's Mitchell. He's got a snake in his hands. A real one. A living one.

"Oh, hiiii," I say, trying to sound calm and casual.

"Oh, hey, Edie." His voice is friendly enough, but he barely looks up as he places the snake in flat plastic tub.

"What are you doing?"

"Just cleaning. I have to take them all out so I can wipe down their enclosures. Come on, Ivan," he says in a gentle voice as he reaches into the next enclosure.

"I was just going over to your house," I say.

"Oh, yeah? What for?"

"Um," I say. Even though I guess it's a normal question, it stings for some reason. My answer comes out like a question. "I guess I wanted to return your *sweatshirt*?"

"Oh, cool," he says as he slowly lifts this Ivan creature out of its enclosure. Ivan's head and upper body are free to poke around. The snake finds the sleeve of Mitchell's T-shirt and noses it curiously.

"You can just throw the sweatshirt over the gate," Mitchell says to me.

The gate. It's five steps closer to him—*and* five steps closer to the snakes. I want to approach, yet I want to retreat. Oh, the paradox!

I take those five steps. I hang his sweatshirt over the gate. He barely looks up. I guess he's busy with Ivan and Imelda and friends, but he's acting so strangely.

"So, uh, did you get in trouble or something?" I ask.

"For what?"

Ouch. There's no way he could have forgotten.

"The other night?" My voice goes high on the "night," giving it a weird inflection. My arms cross protectively in front of my chest.

"Oh." He finally glances at me. "No."

"You said it was a—" Should I wink? Should I do something heavy lidded? I realize I'm not even sure what that really looks like. This must be covered in an advanced flirting lesson. "A *good night.*"

"Yeah, it was great." He throws a little dimple-less smile in my direction.

I try to smile back, but my face does this little spasm instead. "I thought we had fun."

"Yeah, totally. I'm glad we're buds."

Buds. Like buddies. Pals. Chums.

"Yeah, *uh.*" I force the corners of my mouth to inch upward. "Me too."

"How about you? Did you get in trouble?" he asks.

"Uh, no. There was, *uh* . . . a broken toilet."

"A *what?*"

"A . . . *uh* . . ." *Why am I even talking?* "Everyone was just too busy dealing with house issues to really notice I was gone. Things falling apart and stuff."

"Oh, got it," he says. "Well, I guess I better get back to work."

195

"Yeah, me too," I say.

We say bye, and I leave him and his precious serpents alone. Maybe I *should* stick with made-up boyfriends, like Klaus, who I'm sure wouldn't require any flirty talk or special glances—just a no-nonsense smile from time to time. A firm handshake might equally suffice.

Rae and I are in our room. It's late, but our light is still on. She's blabbering on about something. I'm inserting a "yeah" from time to time, along with the occasional "*hmm.*"

"Are you really listening to me?" she asks.

"Yes," I say.

"What was I talking about, then?"

"Leo," I say, which is pretty much a no-brainer.

"What about him?"

I try to remember a few verbal scraps. "That he looks like Justin Timberlake."

"Edie!" She seems exasperated. "You're not listening."

"Okay, I'm sorry, I'm sorry," I say. She opens her mouth, no doubt ready to give me her *Love Story* quote again, but before she can, I add, "I guess I just have a lot on my mind."

"Yeah, I guess I can tell. What's wrong?"

You mean besides the fact that you're on your phone all the time? And Mitchell is so . . . I don't know. And that my best friend is off at camp with my archnemesis? And that visiting day is only three days away and I have yet to get a single checkmark on Petunia's list of good ideas?

"Okay, talk to me, Edie. Does this have something to do with your"—she says the word very carefully—"*boyfriend?*"

"*Nooo.*"

"You've hardly even mentioned him lately."

"I know. It's just that he's just acting weird. He thinks—"

"Hang on. So you actually *talked* to him? When?"

Carp. She means Klaus. Ugh.

"Oh my god, you're talking about Mitchell! I *knew* it! I knew you liked him!"

"No, no!" I stammer. "You've been kind of teasing me about Mitchell all summer, so I thought *that's* who you meant."

"Edie, please. I can see the way you've been looking at him."

"How do I look at him?"

"Like you don't care two poops about Klaus."

Well, there's probably some truth to that.

"Just tell me what's really going on," she says.

I look over at her. She's taken out her contacts and swept her long, flowing hair back. With her glasses, retainer, and ponytail, she looks less like a celebrity, and more like—well, more like a dorky Posey. Which feels like a good thing right now.

I take a deep breath and find it surprisingly gratifying to just finally feel like I can tell her *something*. Even if it's not everything. "It just felt like . . . he liked me a little. And I felt like that back. But then, when I went to give him his sweatshirt, he called me his *bud*. Like he didn't like me like that anymore. Or ever."

"Oh. Okay." She's quiet for a few moments, like something's wrong all over again.

Wait. Could it be that . . . "Rae? Do *you* like Mitchell?"

"No, Edie," she says, and sighs. "And if that's what you think—well, I don't even know where to start."

"Okay, okay," I say, surrendering.

"So is that it? That's all you were going to say? Just that weird stuff with Mitchell?"

Isn't that enough? "Well, yeah, it's just . . . I don't know. Odd."

Then she says, "'Tis better to be brief than tedious."

Oh. Shakespeare, methinks. Sometimes I wish she'd drop the theatrics and just play the part of a caring friend-slash-cousin.

"Shakespeare again?" I ask.

"You know what? That may be Shakespeare, but I'm actually quoting Leo, okay? If you would listen—"

Oh. Leo, of course. I should have guessed.

She snaps off the light. There seems to be a new distance

between us, and I want to close it up somehow.

I wonder if I should just tell her the truth about Klaus now. You know, seize the moment. *Really* seize it. I wait a few minutes, hoping to get the nerve up to get rid of this stupid lie. It would be a matter of four single words, four tiny syllables. *I made him up.* Anyone could do it. You just open your mouth and speak. Like most of this fear-conquering stuff, it's a lot simpler than your head wants to make it.

I take a deep breath. I open my mouth. I—

A hand springs to her heart. Her voice broadens, lifts. "Come, gentle night, come, black-browed night. Give me my Romeo."

"Rae?"

She doesn't answer.

I open my mouth again to speak anyway, but the words completely escape me. I find myself without a line and without an audience. I roll over and wait for the low-tide sound of her breath, hoping it will help lull me to sleep.

Chapter 18

Wake Up

"*G*irls?"

That's the sound that wakes me up.

"*Girls!* It's quite *late!*"

A wake-up visit from my mom. It's more alarming than an actual alarm clock.

I tell my mom we'll be right down.

"Are you feeling okay?"

"Yes, Mom, we're just tired."

"I guess we *have* been working you both pretty hard," my mom says. "Tell you what—how about you two work on the downstairs bathroom today, and then you can have some free time?"

"Free time?" I ask.

"Yes, but work first, free time later. I really need that grout scrubbed clean."

Once she closes the door, I sit up and look over at Rae. She's in her bed, facing away from me. I'm hoping I can just chalk up last night to some of her usual theatrical mood swings. "Raaaaaaae," I say. "Oh, *Raaaaaaae*. Did you hear her? We're free!"

She hums an ambiguous answer.

I try again. This time, I sing. "Free-*dom*! Free-*dom*!" I smile at her. "Well, after the grout, that is."

"Just—please, Edie! Let me sleep ten more minutes," she snaps, and places a pillow over her head.

"Fine," I say, and slip out of the room.

She can sleep as long as she wants to, as far as I'm concerned. Or rather, she can sleep as long as she *can*. And if Beatrice ends up being especially loud this morning, playing with Albert/Odysseus ("Odysseus sees a squirrel." "WOOF WOOF WOOF!" "Odysseus, there's a robber in the house!" "WOOF WOOF CHOMP!") . . . well then, so be it.

Still, I end up hushing the twins. Still, I end up wishing she'd come down.

Half an hour later, I creep back upstairs. I knock softly on the door. No answer.

I push the door. It creaks open. "Rae?"

"Hmm?"

"It's ten."

"That's nice." She's lying on her back now, but she doesn't open her eyes.

"Rae?"

But all she says is "One may smile, and smile, and be a villain."

"Why are you reciting Shakespeare?" I ask.

"I'm just—I don't know. Forget it," she says, exhaling. "So what did you want?"

"Well, uh . . . I've got a great idea for our free time."

She pops open one eye. "What's your idea?"

"Item six. Write something scary." It's the first thing on Petunia's list that seems to involve more brains than guts. It should come naturally to me—something I could actually succeed at, unlike everything else.

As I could have predicted, she says, "How is that postable?"

But I've practically rehearsed my answer. I sit down on my couch bed. "Okay, listen. What if we write a really scary story—like something truly terrifying? A ghost story, maybe. Something really haunting. And when we've finished writing it, we could post it online somewhere. How postable is *that*? Maybe we can even make our own blog!"

She sighs. "I don't know, Edie."

I feel unsure about what's wrong, and even more unsure about how to make it right. "What's the matter?" I ask.

"Maybe I'm getting a little bored with the whole list thing."

"Bored?" That word gets me again. I can still hear Sophi's voice: *"Don't you think she's boring?"* Even though I'm as far away from boring as I've ever been, it feels like I'll never be far enough.

She curls up on her bed. "Well, I don't know. Maybe I've just been away for too long. Maybe I just miss my real life. Maybe that's all it is."

"Oh." I feel her words in the pit of my stomach. Her real life. Her real friends.

I guess my hurt feelings show on my face, because she looks at me and says, "I didn't mean . . . sorry, Edie, I guess I'm just grumpy."

"You just said I was boring."

"No, I said *it* was boring. The list. But never mind what I said, okay? Maybe I do miss my life, but sometimes?" She lifts her chin. Her voice is rich and smooth. "Sometimes I wish I could take you back there with me."

There's something about the grand way she says it that gives me an uncomfortable thought. "I wish I could take you all home with me." It's like she's a movie star speaking to a crowd of fans.

Does Rae want a friend, or does she want a *fan*?

I immediately want to erase that thought. I don't want to claim it.

"Edie, don't worry, I know the list matters to you, so let's just do it. Okay?" She looks at me in an apologetic way.

I hesitate, still a little hurt, but mostly relieved. "Okay." At least she's still in this with me. At least I can get a checkmark. At least I won't be boring for too much longer.

We've scrubbed the grout to an admirable white-beige in the downstairs bathroom—or mostly, I have, while Rae's spent a lot of time reclining in the empty clawfoot tub and texting her beasties, but I figure I have to put up with a little of that if I want her to work on the list with me. But when I've finished and I'm ready to work on our story, Rae is nowhere to be found.

I look out the bathroom window, but I don't see her outside. I go out to both the front and back porches and check around, and still, no luck. Back inside, our parents are in the kitchen. My dad is going on and on about the concept of Roman blinds—okay, the *history* of them—but I don't think anyone's listening. My mom and uncle are hunched over a pile of receipts.

"Has anyone seen Rae?"

"Thought I heard her upstairs," my uncle says.

I go back upstairs, but our room is empty. I pop my head into the twins' room.

"Guess what, Edith," Beatrice says when she sees me. "I saw my kitten last night."

"It's not *your* kitten," Henry says. "Edith, would you please tell her that a stray cat doesn't belong to anyone?"

I ignore the request. "Have you guys seen Rae?"

Now they ignore me. "When an Egyptian cat died, its owners shaved their own eyebrows to show how sad they were," Beatrice says.

"That makes no sense," Henry declares.

I sigh and try again. "Hey, you guys, have you—" I hear the back door slam, and our parents greeting Rae. "Never mind."

I go downstairs and meet Rae in the hall.

"Hey," she says.

"Hey," I say. "Where were you?"

"Out there, trying to call Leo."

"I looked outside. I didn't see you."

She shrugs. "I mean out there in the shed. You know that's where my phone works best."

"Oh, yeah," I say. But every time she looks at me, her eyes flit away. So I ask, "Is everything okay?"

"Yeah, I mean, I guess." She scratches the back of her head. "I actually couldn't get ahold of him."

"Oh. But you were gone so long—"

"Because I kept trying," she says, in a tone that sounds like an admission of defeat. "Anyway, I thought you wanted to work on that story."

"Yeah, I do," I say.

"So let's do it," she says.

But once we go into the study, it's clear that her heart's still not in it. "Once upon a time . . . there was this ogre. Who lived in a swamp. And one day, his kingdom was invaded—"

"Isn't that *Shrek*?" I ask.

"Yeah, I guess it is. Okay, how about this? Once upon a time there was a scientist. And he decides to create a monster—"

"Really, Rae? *Frankenstein*?"

She tilts her head and looks at me. "I see dead people?"

Another movie line, I'm sure. I tilt my head back at her.

She sighs. "I'm just not that good at this, Edie."

"But Rae," I say, "I know you'd be good at this if you'd just try."

"Well, then, I'm just not in the mood for this."

"How can that even be? You love movies—you love plays. You love *stories*."

"Honestly, Edie." Rae stares at me. "I'm just so sick of stories. I wish *some people* would just tell the truth."

I swallow, thinking about our conversation last night. "Is this about Klaus?"

"You mean your imaginary boyfriend?"

Carp! She knows!

"How long have you known?" My voice comes out quiet.

"You basically told me last night."

"I'm sorry, Rae. It was a really stupid lie," I say. "I feel like such an idiot."

"No, I'm the idiot! I mean, who has a boyfriend named Klaus?"

There *is* that.

"I guess I just wanted you to like me, so . . . don't be mad?" I realize my plea sounds like a question.

"Look, Edie, we're friends, right? Like real friends?" She has a look on her face that I recognize, though it looks unfamiliar on her. Tense eyebrows, worried eyes. *Wounded.*

"Yes, Rae, of course!"

"Well, then don't do that kind of stuff to me. Don't pretend to be someone you're not."

"Okay," I say weakly. "Sorry."

Her shoulders seem to relax, and she releases a breath. "Look, let's just forget about Klaus. Deal?"

I will happily forget about Klaus, who, as of late, I've come to think of as having a constantly dripping nose and a strangely large bottom. "Deal," I say.

She cracks a weary smile. "Look, Edie, you can keep working on your scary story if you want. I give up. I'm going to take a nap."

"But . . . what do you mean you give up? You're not giving up on the list, are you?"

She lifts her eyebrows and looks at me.

"I just mean, what about crossing the swamp and stuff, like Petunia did? Item seven? Next Sunday night is the last full moon of the summer. It could be fun."

She sighs. "I'll do the rest of the things on the list with you, Edie. I'm just over this one, okay?"

I smile, relieved. "Okay."

"Anyway, that's not until Sunday. Tomorrow . . . I think we should go bird-watching tomorrow with the dizygotes. What do you think?"

"You want to go *bird-watching*?" I wonder if she knows how much watching, waiting, recording, and observing that involves. It's kind of the opposite of all that seizing she likes to do.

"Yeah, why not?" She shrugs. "I'm tired of being stuck at the house all the time."

Why not? Because tomorrow is visiting day and Taylor is calling—being stuck at the house is exactly where I want to be. So I can't say I caught a snake, or flirted with a boy, or danced in a hurricane, but I can say I'm writing a story—or, wait, a whole book, with an ending! I bet Sophi Angelo can't write anything more than a text message!

"I've spent every single day of my life with the twins," I say. "You go ahead. I'll stay here and work on the story."

"Okay, then." Rae says bye, and leaves.

I fidget with the pen and begin to pace around the study, trying my best to come up with something really scary: mysteries, monsters, ghosts, poltergeists—bring it on! I can handle it! Can't I? *Can I?*

But the more I try to dream it up, the more I realize I don't have to. Who says this *something scary* has to be fiction? Real life can be scary enough.

I sit back down and begin to write.

Chapter 19

Apple Tree

Visiting day.

My eyes pop wide open. Our room seems particularly quiet. I sit up, look around, and realize I'm alone. The bird-watching party must have gotten an early start.

Downstairs in the kitchen, Uncle A.J. is putting in a new sink faucet. "Hey, there, Edie. Give me a hand?"

He has me hold the faucet above the sink while he goes inside the cabinet and wrenches it tight at the base. When he's done, we stand back and take a moment to admire it. It's one of those tall gooseneck-looking faucets. "Thought your dad was crazy at first, but now I got to admit. It was a good choice."

"Yeah, it was," I say.

He looks at me. "Didn't feel like joining the search for that endangered bird this morning?"

"The scrub jay," I say. "No, I didn't. It could actually take forever."

"Well, you may be right—your dad did seem determined to find it. But that suits me fine," he says. "We've got a lot to do still, and with everyone out of our hair, maybe we can get it done. Your mom's upstairs replacing some drywall, and I have to install that new toilet."

I can't believe I'm going to ask this. "Do you want me to help or anything?"

"No, Edie." He gives me a great big bear hug of a smile. "I think you should just enjoy some downtime."

I grab some coffee, and Uncle A.J. hands me a Pop-Tart— with a finger to his lips—before he heads back upstairs.

I wander back into the study and take a look at the story I finished last night, titled "Ophidian." It's a word I found in Petunia's thesaurus, a word for snakelike.

Last night, the word felt like a stroke of genius; today, it seems a little melodramatic.

I read on, remembering how stressful it felt last night to

relive the event from my childhood—it involved a lot of deep breaths of the three-counts-in, four-counts-out variety.

I was six when my dad took me to the zoo and I witnessed my first murder.

My dad and I were at the snake house, learning all about the different places snakes live—wet places and dry places, hot places and cool places—and how well they can hide. In some of the habitats, we couldn't even see the snakes, no matter how hard we looked.

We stopped at the anaconda cage. Even though the snake was huge, we had to get very close to the glass to see it. It was lurking in its little pond, trying to hide under the murky surface, waiting for its feeding time.

Then a zoo worker entered the cage, holding a rabbit. Suddenly, the snake struck out of the water and sank its fangs into the rabbit before wrapping its gigantic body around it. Everyone around us swarmed in, and I was pressed toward the front of the crowd, practically into the glass of the enclosure—forced to witness the murder up close!

I remember my dad hugging me and telling me that the rabbit was already dead when the snake attacked it. But still, in my mind, the damage had been done. Snakes were the enemy, and they were everywhere—trees, lakes, ponds, deserts. Hiding. Waiting. Ready to attack. Suddenly, the world seemed a lot less safe.

But now I look down at the words I have on the page, and the whole thing feels a bit ridiculous. *Witness? Murder?* Is this really what's been making me so scared all these years? Feeding time at the zoo?

This is my scary story? *Carp!* What will I tell—

My thoughts are interrupted by a shrill ring.

TAYLOR?

I grab the phone before the first ring is even finished.

"Hi, hi!" Ugh. I sound just like Colvin. "I mean . . . hello?"

The line is quiet.

"Taylor?" I say.

"Is this— Edie, is that you?" a distinctively *not*-Taylor voice asks. "This is Officer Elwayne. How are you doing, my friend?"

"I'm . . ." *Incredibly disappointed yet oddly relieved, of course.* "Fine."

"Glad to hear it. Can I speak to one of your parents?"

I put the receiver down and go to call up the stairs. "Mom! Officer Elwayne's on the phone for you!"

"Okay, I'll get it up here!" she calls down to me.

The ceiling above me creaks, and I wait to hear her "Hello?"

I return to the study, but instead of hanging up the

receiver, I find myself listening in.

Officer Elwayne is talking. "—wanted to check in. I think we got another mistaken alligator sighting."

"Oh? Where was it reported?" My mom sounds the teensiest bit worried.

"Well, the caller was farther down the road from you, not far from the Amoses' house. But when Rosie and I got there, it was just that roaming iguana of Petunia's."

"You mean Barbara?" my mom asks.

"Sure. Happens sometimes," Officer Elwayne says. "People drive by, see something green and scaly poking around in the grass—they think it's a gator. But I tell you, if there was an alligator around, there probably wouldn't be an iguana moseying around chewing on grass. She'd already have been lunch."

They have a nice little chuckle over that.

"So nothing to worry about, then," my mom says.

"None that I can tell, but these false reports are starting to become a real head-scratcher. Just let me know if you see anything strange."

"We certainly will," my mom promises.

They begin to chitchat about the house, and I'm starting to feel impatient. What if Taylor calls? I let out a frustrated sigh before I realize that they might hear me.

"Edith?" my mom says. "Are you still on the line?"

I close my mouth.

"Sorry, I thought she might have forgotten to hang it up," my mom says to Officer Elwayne.

He lets out a snicker. "Watch out for that one. She sure is a sweet girl, but the apple doesn't fall far from the tree."

Something about his mischievous tone makes me think of the night he brought us home from the hurricane. *"My old friend Hannah."* And then I have another memory. Welles. *"Wild as a thicket of blackberries."*

A few minutes later, after we've all hung up, I hear the floorboards of the stairs squeak, and my mom tries to walk nonchalantly past the study.

"Mom?"

She stops walking.

"I actually was listening."

She makes a *tsk* sound. "Well, that's called eavesdropping, Edith, and—"

"I know, okay? And I'm sorry. But what did he mean by that last thing he said?"

"By what, honey?"

I tilt my head and look at her. "The apple not falling far from the tree. Because I'm guessing that this is about me sneaking out the night he brought us home. I'm the apple and you're the tree, aren't you?"

She seems to shrink. "Okay, Edith."

I wait for her to continue. When she doesn't, I say, "Well?"

"*Well.*" Her exhale sounds like a slow leak, and like a raft she seems to deflate. "The fact is that I had my share of antics when I was a teenager."

"Antics?"

"Like, well, also sneaking out. And having Officer Elwayne bring me home."

"You *did*? I don't believe it."

"Edith, I'm not proud of it, and you shouldn't be either."

I smirk. "What else?"

"Well, a lot of skipping school. In fact, so much that I was this close to failing ninth grade." She pinches her thumb and forefinger together so close that they almost touch.

"No, you—you couldn't have. You're . . . well, you're *you*. With a Ph.D.! In statistics! You don't fail anything. You might even be the smartest person I know!"

"Thank you, Edith, but doing well in school isn't necessarily the same as being smart." She comes in and sits down in a chair in front of the desk. "I guess I took a lot of silly risks when I was young."

"At least Petunia let you take them."

"It's more that she didn't try to stop me. I did a lot of things just to try to get her attention. Sometimes I felt like she cared more about her animals than she did me."

"But . . . that can't be right," I say. "Maybe she loved you so much that she wanted you to have your freedom. Like the way she handled Barbara. You know, maybe she was worried about 'killing your spirit.'"

She seems to consider it. "Well, Edith, I suppose that's possible. But I think I needed more of a mom, less of a handler." She smiles a little at me. "Maybe that's why I hang on so tight sometimes. I never want you to feel that way."

"Oh." I feel a little stupid at always being so upset with my mom.

"I *am* sorry you didn't get to meet her, Edith." She smiles. "You probably would have liked her."

"I *do* like her," I say.

My mom lifts her eyebrows.

"I kind of feel like I know her—just being here, you know, and meeting people who knew her."

She gives me a sad smile. "I wish she and I had worked out our problems. But—and you'll hear this a lot as you get older—relationships aren't always easy. They can really get complicated."

I think about what she says, and the fact that Rae is out bird-watching and I'm here without her. And Mitchell— well. That's even more complicated, with all that *bud* stuff. And then, of course, there's Taylor and all those scary things that I don't even know what to do with. Yes, relationships really aren't easy. I have a summerload of proof of that.

"Mom?" I say this even though she's already looking at me.
"Yes?"

"Taylor's been with Sophi at Camp Berrybrook all summer. They've been hanging out together nonstop."

"Oh." She grimaces.

"And I picked up the phone because she was supposed to call me today—it's visiting day and her mom was going to make sure she called me. But she hasn't."

"Oh, no. I'm so sorry, honey. I didn't know any of this. Is that who you're writing to?"

I look down at my page. "No, this is just—" *Another failed checkmark.* "Something else."

"Well, maybe you *should* write to her." She lets out a long sigh, one that sounds a lot like relief. "Sometimes it feels better to get things out there."

Then she tells me she's going to make some coffee and asks if I want a cup. *One* cup.

Now it's my turn to confess. "To tell the truth, I've been sneaking it all summer."

"Oh, I know. I've been keeping tabs."

"And you let me?"

She smiles in a way that makes me feel a little more grown-up. Or at least more *almost thirteen*, and less twelve. I take her up on that cup of coffee.

She gives me a little head squeeze of a hug and leaves me

to writing. But I think about what she said, and crumple up my story. What scares me most—it's not snakes.

It's losing the one person I look forward to seeing every day, the one person who truly understands me. It's lonely Saturday nights. It's making new friends. Forget flirting and dancing in abandoned buildings. Sure, those things have freaked me out, but it's losing Taylor that scares me the most, and maybe, like my mom said, it will feel better to just get it out there.

I try this scary thing again.

Dear Taylor.

Wait. I cross it out. Too serious. Too brooding.

Taylor, hey you!

Too flippant. This time I tear the sheet off the tablet.

Hi, Taylor—

There's something I need to tell you.

I stop again. Now what? I tell her how I've spent the summer doing all these crazy things just so I wouldn't lose her to Sophi Angelo? And she doesn't even know it?

I feel a jolt of panic. Who am I fooling? She's been off gallivanting with Sophi at Camp Berrybrook for almost a month. The scary-awful truth is that the worst thing has probably already happened—I've probably already lost her. And if I haven't, none of the stuff I've done or *haven't* done is going to keep her interested in me.

This letter is useless. Pathetic. Ridiculous.

But the list? It's just become more important. Because suddenly it has nothing to do with proving anything to Taylor. And it has everything to do with proving something to myself.

I *will* cross Corkscrew Swamp. Under that full moon. Which will be rising on Sunday night.

I've been helping my mom and uncle out all afternoon—it seemed like they could use it. It's pretty late in the day when Rae and the twins burst in from their day-cation. I'm in the upstairs hall taping over a patch of new drywall when I hear the thud of the back door, and then the twins laughing their heads off like they've had the time of their lives.

"Edith?" Beatrice calls out.

"I'm upstairs!"

They flop and thwack their way up the stairs, and I notice their hair and clothes are damp.

"Um, last I checked, the Florida scrub jay is a bird, not a fish," I joke.

"It still is," Henry says.

"Oh! We spent almost four hours just filming, waiting for it, but *nothing*," Rae says. "So then we decided to jump into the lake. And guess what, Edie? Already a hundred and ninety-four likes! And everyone thinks the supertwins are really"—she sort of winks—*"smart* as a button."

"Yeah, we did carpe diem!"

So now Beatrice is saying it too?

"You don't *do* carpe diem," Henry corrects Beatrice. "You just carpe diem. Right, Rae?"

"Right."

The twins run off to their room to change, and Rae and I go into ours.

"So, drywall?" Rae says as she flops down on her bed, damp clothes and all. "*That's* what you've been doing all day? I thought you wanted to work on your story."

"Yeah, I *did* work on it."

"So can I read it?"

"It's mostly in my head," I say.

"Oh," she says. "I thought you wanted to check something off that list."

"I did. I do," I say. "I mean, I tried, but—let's just focus on Sunday night."

"What's Sunday night?" she asks.

"The full moon."

She looks at me blankly.

"*Rae,*" I say, trying to hide my simmering annoyance. "Item seven. Cross Corkscrew Swamp under a full moon? And you said—"

"Oh. Right!" she says. "I remember. I said I'd do it with you."

"Because I need you to—"

I stop. Now what exactly do I need her for? Am I too scared to do this on my own, or is this just another case where I've made things so much scarier in my head than they are in reality?

"I know, I get it. We have to sneak out, and get to the swamp in the dark, and then—wait, have you ever rowed a boat?"

"No," I admit.

"Well, I have," she says. Of course she has. "The oars can get heavy. It's a little hard at first, but you get used to it, so it's not, you know, impossible."

I sigh and deflate. Like it or not, I do need her.

Chapter 20

Corked

It's Sunday evening. The moon is full. And I don't want anything to ruin the plan tonight. Not Rae's flagging enthusiasm and increasing absences. Not the constant interruption of all things Leo, and all things "like"-able. Not the fact that everything feels like it's changing in some way, like a day being deprived of a few seconds.

The furniture—at least what's being kept to stage the house—has been moved into the center of the room and covered with canvas, and Rae and I are painting the study. Our arms are sore from using the paint rollers; our skin is splattered with specks of du jour white.

Uncle A.J. checks in on us. "How's it going, sports?"

"Horrible," Rae says. "I thought you weren't supposed to paint on a rainy day."

"It's just drizzling. And anyway, that sounds like some sort of superstition," he says.

"No, actually, paint takes longer to dry on a rainy day," I say, and then immediately shut up. I sound so Posey-Preston.

Uncle A.J. laughs. "Well, if we had all the time in the world, maybe we could wait. But fact is, we're running out of it. So paint on."

He leaves, and Rae says, "Now *he's* hovering."

"Yeah, I think my mom might actually be contagious," I say, and sigh. "I just hope they're working as hard as they're making *us* work. Maybe they'll sleep like babies tonight."

"Yeah, that'd be good," she says. Her voice is a little flat, but she's been so moody lately, it doesn't really surprise me.

"So," I say, "I checked on the rowboat while you were—well, what were you doing?"

"When?" she asks.

"When you sort of disappeared this morning."

"Oh, well, I was trying to call Leo."

"Again?"

She looks a little embarrassed. And maybe she should be. She's always calling him.

"Anyway," I continue, "everything's ready. I . . ." *I walked down to the swamp all by myself!* I can't say that. I'd sound like a kindergartner. And of course I was making all sorts of kissing noises. And I might have tiptoed and run as fast as I possibly could, like some sort of scurrying mouse-human. So maybe I should just keep it to myself. "I mean, the rowboat is ready to go."

"Oh, okay. Cool."

"We'll need our flashlights. And you'll probably want to wear your black sweatshirt—or something dark like that."

"Okay." She keeps rolling the wall with the paint.

Her roller seems a bit dry, so I pour some more paint into the tray and offer it to her. "Do you want—"

But she's hardly paying attention, and she answers the question I haven't dared to ask. "Yes, I *told* you I'd go with you, Edie."

"I meant do you want some more paint on that roller?"

Then she finally notices I'm holding the paint tray.

"Oh." She lets out a weak laugh. "Sorry."

"It's okay," I say. And I want that to be true—that everything is actually okay. So I put on a voice as flowery and dramatic as I can muster. "Love means never having to say you're sorry. Right?"

She brightens. "Oh my god, Edie. That's right. *Love Story.* You really *are* getting good at this."

Or maybe I'm just getting pretty used to it. The same way Petunia got used to having her mouth washed out with soap.

I prefer Ivory.

But she lets out a laugh, and I make myself smile back, because I want to believe in the dynamic duo again. Like nothing between us has changed.

But apparently something has. Because at dinner at the BEST Diner in Town, Rae says, "I have to go to the bathroom."

"Okay," I say.

She lowers her chin. "No, I mean *we* have to go to the bathroom."

"Oh. Okay." But instead of feeling a sense of togetherness, I feel a sense of dread.

In the bathroom, Rae takes a breath and says, "So I have to tell you something."

"What?" I try not to let it sound like an accusation, but it probably does.

"Don't hate me." She bites her bottom lip.

"You're canceling on me, aren't you? *Unbelievable.*"

"No, Edie. I'm *not*, okay? But I might be a little late."

"Why?"

"You're going to think I'm so stupid. It's—"

"Is it Leo?"

She stares at the floor. "If you must know . . . ," she says, and then stops.

"What?"

"If you must know." She meets my eyes, sighs, and looks down again. "Leo is FaceTiming me. I have to go out to the shed to take his call, since it's the only place I have good reception."

I exhale. "How late are you going to be?"

"I don't know. Maybe an hour? It's our six-month-iversary. And okay, Edie, to be honest, he's been kind of hard to reach lately. But he wanted to make sure I could talk with him tonight—"

"Month-iversary?" I'm sure I sound disgusted. If this is what having a real boyfriend is really all about, maybe I'll go back to the fake ones. And just stick to *buds*.

"See?" She looks hurt. "I knew you'd think it was stupid."

I don't correct her—she's not wrong. I just push the door open and head back to our table. Once there, I wedge myself in between Henry and Beatrice and play a million rounds of tic-tac-toe—enough to numb my brain. I feel Rae staring at me from time to time, but I don't look at her, not once.

And although we sit next to each other in the van on the way back from dinner as usual, I sit as far away from her as possible. When we hit a bump in the road and my ankle accidentally touches hers, I pull it quickly away.

Chapter 21

Knock Knock

The house is completely quiet. After saying good night to everyone and pretending to come to bed, Rae snuck out to the shed to take her stupid month-iversary FaceTime call. But it's been over an hour, and I'm flopping around on my couch bed on this last full moon of our stay—which has turned out to be incredibly bright after all—feeling like I'm letting a critical opportunity pass by.

Mitchell.

His name pops into my mind, and I sit up in bed. Never mind Rae and her precious Leo. Maybe Mitchell will come with me, friend or *bud* or whatever he is.

I quickly get out of bed and feel around for my clothes

and shoes. After I dress, I run my fingers through my hair and tiptoe down the hall.

I pause in front of the twins' bedroom door and hold my breath. But I don't hear a thing—not a rustle, not a whisper. I'm safe from their prying eyes. I continue my slow creep down the stairs. Through the kitchen. Out the back door.

Outside, I stop. My hands are empty. I've forgotten the flashlight! But I can't risk going back, and the brightness of the moon lights the path ahead. It seems like there's nowhere to go but forward.

I move into a fast shuffle across the yard. *Smack. Smack. Smack.* I make the snake-clearing kissing noises as I run toward Mitchell's house. I'm relieved to see that the lights are still on, and I can hear the sound of the TV as I get closer. I also smell something baking—cookies, maybe?

I knock, but the TV's pretty loud. I hear an Italian-accented voice. *The Godfather?*

I try again, but some talking and a burst of laughter from inside drowns it out.

If I didn't know better, I'd think a party was going on. Old Edith would have tucked her tail and gone home, but now, I just knock harder.

"Hey, Mitchell?"

"Edie?" I hear. The laughing stops. The TV is turned down. "Hang on a sec, okay?"

When the door opens, he gives me an awkward smile. "Hey. How's it going?"

"It's—" I stop myself. I don't want to get caught up in small talk and lose my nerve, so I just Geronimo my way into the invitation. "I wanted to ask you—"

But then I notice something. A pair of flip-flops. Hot pink. Rae's. And it all makes sense. Rae's disappearing acts. Mitchell's weirdness. *The Godfather.* They've been secretly hanging out together and haven't wanted to tell me.

I've been a complete moron.

"What did you want to ask me about?"

Uh, uh, *uh*. "Turtles," I say quickly. Once again, it's clear that I don't think well on the spot. Klaus. Toilets. Turtles. Wonderful.

"Turtles?" he asks.

I shake my head. "Never mind," I say, backing off the porch. "I'll just see you around."

"Edie?" he says, but I turn and start walking away.

Then I hear *her* voice. "You think she knew I was here?"

Mitchell's answer is muffled, but I hear Rae say something that makes me feel like I'm dying a little inside. She says, "I guess I should just tell her."

Great. I look forward to it. The two of them, holding hands, declaring their undying love for each other. I'm sure there will be some *Romeo and Juliet* flung about—Rae will insist on that. *How romantic.*

I've been feeling bad about inventing Klaus, but she's probably been lying to me all summer. Should I be surprised? She's an actor. The summer's been one grand performance. And for Rae, all the world's a stage.

I think Shakespeare said that, too.

I sit on the porch, feeling incredibly alone. I've been betrayed by Rae and Mitchell, forgotten about by Taylor. I almost wish that Klaus *was* real. As lumpy and pale and big bottomed as he's become in my head, I just want a friend to call on. I want *someone* to be on my side.

Petunia.

I sigh. Okay, there's Petunia, sure. It's her list. She'd be cheering me on. But I would like very much for that person to be alive.

And she's not.

But I am. And I've done a lot of things this summer—things that once scared me. Even if everything hasn't gone as planned, it feels like maybe someday, not so far over the rainbow, I'll go camping. At the lake. And dive headfirst into the water at night. And talk to high school boys. And do other brave, bold, fearless things.

But if so, I shouldn't be sitting alone on the porch, feeling sorry for myself—no self-respecting adventurer would be.

She'd strap up her boots and embark upon the journey on her own.

I stand up, though my knees are wobbly; I straighten up, though my body wants to shrink. And I take my first step into the dark, unknown night.

Chapter 22

Swamped

I am approaching Corkscrew Swamp, my heart intent on crossing in the rowboat.

Well, truthfully, my heart is slightly more intent on being safely tucked away in my bed. But telling myself otherwise helps me feel a little more like a brave explorer than the scaredy-cat I really am, particularly at this moment.

I hear something shuffle in the tall grasses not far from me and freeze—a scream stuck in the base of my throat. I charge on. Or try to. But it's like my body has been sprayed with glue. My arms attach tightly to my ribs, and my legs squeeze together as I walk. It's hardly the heroic march that I imagined. I am aware, all of a sudden, that I'm not breathing, which is something that I must do in order to stay upright and not become anaconda bait.

I force myself to draw in a deep, boggy breath of thick swamp air. I take another step, but my boot sinks an inch into the muddy ground. As I try for another step forward, my heel almost slips out of the boot. I tug at the boot to remove it from the mud. With a wet, slurping sound, my boot is liberated, and I spot the rowboat, belly up, about ten feet in front of me.

Which is not how I left it earlier.

Clearly, someone was here after my trip here this morning. Someone has tampered with my carefully laid-out plans. For a few seconds, I think about turning around and giving in to that safe-in-bed intent, but the scene looks more sloppy than sinister. Besides, Gutsy Edie wouldn't dream of such a thing.

I splosh through the mud toward the rowboat. When I reach it, I hook my fingers under the edge. It's heavier than I expected, and the more I try to lift it, the more my feet sink, and I slip into the mud with a shriek that embarrasses me, even without an audience.

After struggling with the slimy terrain, I make my way back to my feet, using about nine muscles I never knew I had. I dig the heels of my boots into the mud. This time, I'm prepared. Again, I grip the rim of the rowboat. With a giant exhale, I flip the boat over. Then I begin to push it the short distance back to the edge of the swamp.

"There," I say. For some reason, it feels better to say it out loud, like I'm with a friend. But the only response is the wind whipping through the trees—why does that always sound so spooky in the dark?—and the rustle of branches and grass.

I shake it off—fine, I'll embrace it. I'm the lone adventurer, and that's okay. In fact, that's more than okay. That makes me even more of an intrepid pioneer.

But wait. There's only one oar. *Where would the other be?* I wipe the lenses of my glasses and scan the moonlit ground. Nothing. I turn around to survey the area behind me. But although my eyes register nothing that will help me cross the swamp, my ears go on full alert.

Footsteps. Quiet. Slinking. Stealth-like. Leopard-like. Toward me.

Wait. Are there leopards in Florida?

I freeze again. And then I hear a whisper. Two whispers. I am not alone, and I've never before wanted to be alone quite like this.

"I can hear you!" I call out in my meanest voice.

Silence.

The whispers come again. But this time I can make out the words.

"See us . . . doing here . . . should."

It's the Posey-Preston *should* that gives it away.

The air sweeps back into my lungs. *"Twins!"* My voice comes out scolding. My nerves are confused: I'm thawing with relief; I'm simmering with exasperation.

Again, silence.

"Beatrice, Henry." I let out a *grrr* of a sigh. "I know you're there."

Slowly their small figures emerge from the shadows.

Then we all say it together: *"What are you doing here?"*

"Wait!" I add. "You didn't follow me?"

"No," Beatrice says.

"Okay, but you were out here earlier, weren't you? Playing with the boat?"

"What boat?" Henry says.

"Edith, we're just trying to film my kitten," Beatrice says. "He only comes out at night."

"Out here, though? You guys! This isn't safe! A million things could happen!" I don't like how I sound. I take a breath. "Besides, Henry, I thought you didn't believe in this cat."

"I'll believe it if I can see it," Henry says.

"Why are *you* here?" Beatrice asks. She's wearing the glasses tonight. She's in charge.

"Just . . ." I think back to all the reasons that have gotten me here tonight. To keep my best friend. To conquer my fears. To be brave. To be *Edie*. To prove that I can.

"Just for . . . reasons," I say. "You guys really need to go home."

"We'll go home when *you* go home," Beatrice says.

"No, I—"

"Come on, Henry," she says, and they both dart past me toward the rowboat.

Great. My night has been ruined not once, but twice. The only upside is that it can't get much worse.

But they start pushing the rowboat to the very edge of the swamp, and Beatrice jumps into the boat.

"No, no, no, and *no*," I say. "Get out of the boat. No one's going anywhere. It's not safe."

"But we saw you—you flipped it over. *You* were going to go out in it," Henry says.

"Yeah, Edith, why?"

I don't answer—I don't feel like explaining. *It's on a fifty-year-old list of random things our grandmother might have done one summer.* Suddenly, this good idea seems like a really bad one all over again. It's one thing to have my own safety to worry about. But it's another thing to have the fate of two eight-year-old genius-slash-nitwits in your hands.

"Beatrice, out of there! Now!"

"Fine—we'll go home and tell Mom where you are. You'll be in so much trouble!"

"I don't even care about that now, Beatrice. Just get out of the boat!"

Henry looks at me, pauses, and then jumps into the rowboat himself.

"Henry!"

The boat starts sliding into the swamp. I lunge and reach for it, but my fingers only graze the edge and push it farther into the water.

"Okay, look, you two. Just paddle back to me, okay? And I'll get in, and we'll all row out." It's a lie, but this time a necessary one.

Under the moonlight, I can see Henry's face change into an *oh-carp* expression. "I forgot the paddles."

I look down. In the grassy weeds, I see the single oar. Better than nothing. "Here's one. I'll try to float it out to you. Now listen, you've got to be careful. You can't just lean out and grab it. You'll have to reach for it. *Slowly.*"

"No, it won't make it out this far," Henry says. "There's a current."

"Maybe I can grab the other one," Beatrice says.

"Yeah, I can't *find* the other one," I tell her. "That's one of the major issues here."

"I think it's right there. It's floating toward us."

I turn my head. About thirty feet upswamp, there is a slow ripple. Something long is headed in the direction of the canoe.

And it's not an oar.

I can't tell what it is. I squint and try to focus. And then I see the moon shine off two round orbs, just above the surface of the water.

Eyes.

Reptilian eyes.

Fear charges through me like an electric bolt. I gasp, and freeze, and in fractions of a second, a million thoughts—most of them useless—race through my head. *Jump in. Run away. Call nine one one. Scream. Stay quiet. Wake up!*

I grab for the only ones that make sense. And even that might be a stretch.

Take the oar. Climb the tree.

There's a tree with a thick branch bowing over the water. Maybe I can climb it and clock the alligator between the eyes. That's what you do, right? Or is that a shark? *Great*—it's not like I have time to look it up in the encyclopedia!

I tell the twins to be quiet and still.

"Why?" they ask.

I'm thankful for their fuzzy vision, their single pair of shared glasses. They have no idea what awaits.

"Just because." That's the best I can do, and that'll have to be good enough. They seem to sense that they shouldn't continue interrogating. Maybe it's because they see me standing at the base of the tree, with an oar clamped under my arm, wondering how I can magically turn into Tarzan.

I reach for a branch of the tree and try to pull myself up, which is hard to do with the oar clamping going on. My muscles lose; gravity wins. But the fate of my siblings is in my hands!

I try again. This time I grab the low, thick branch and try to kick a leg up and over. But the bark is digging into my fingers; my hands are on fire.

"Edith?" Henry asks in a tiny voice. A tiny, vulnerable voice that belongs to a young child who is unaware that he's about to become an alligator's late-night snack. So much for these waters being too salty.

I don't answer. I *can't* answer. Every ounce of energy I have must be applied toward the twins' survival. This time when I grab the branch, I'm fueled more by will than actual muscle. I swing the rest of myself up and over the branch. Finally, I am in the tree, straddling the branch.

I scoot a little farther out on the branch and take a strong hold of the oar.

Between the eyes, I think.

But this hungry predator has to be twenty feet away, and the oar is only five feet long. If only the alligator was a little closer!

For a second, it hits me that in a million years, I would

never have wished for some alligator to actually be closer to me! Not in *ever*!

I scoot a little farther out on the branch, to try to get a better reach, but it causes me to wobble. I try to regain my balance, clutching the branch with my legs and free arm, but it's too late.

CARP.

The oar plunges into the water, and gravity tips my body sideways. I am grasping the branch for dear life, suspended from the tree like a sloth. Raw, cold, unfiltered fear courses through my body. The alligator bobs a little and ducks partly under the surface of water. It must be preparing for its predatory strike.

Beatrice and Henry are the human hors d'oeuvres. I am the main course. Human shish kebab, conveniently hanging on a skewer just inches above the water's surface.

"Edith!" It's Beatrice's voice, interrupting my silent but frantic prayers. "It's an *alligator!*"

"Cover your eyes!" I yell, and clamp my own shut. *"Don't look!"*

"Edie!" I hear Rae calling my name.

"Rae?" I call out.

"Edie, where are you?"

"No! Don't! *DANGER!*"

I hear the frantic snapping of her flip-flops as she gets closer.

"We're in the boat!" Henry calls out.

The footsteps approach the water. Her flashlight shines on my slothlike body.

"Rae," I say, trying to breathe. If I can't save the twins, or myself, I must at least save her. "Don't come. Any closer!"

But she doesn't listen. I hear ripples in the water, and then a splash.

She has foolishly gone into the water.

This is about to become an alligator's Thanksgiving.

I scream. I fall.

Everything goes cold and black.

Chapter 23

Lumps of Sugar, Grains of Salt

"Would you wake up?" It's Petunia's voice—it has to be. There's a texture to it, like crumbled lumps of sugar. Grainy and sweet. "Please?"

"It's *you*," I say, my eyes trying to flutter open.

"You're not dead!" Petunia says, her voice sounding smoother.

I open an eye and squint to focus. My eyes feel naked without my glasses. A harsh light blinds me. I'm confused. Am I supposed to go *toward* the light, or *away* from it?

"*Edith!*" young voices call out. First in the air around me, then straight into my ear. *Angels? Cherubs?* They're clinging to me, smelling wet and damp. Like swamp water. I guess no one thinks to tell you that angels kind of stink. And then, through my squinty eye, I notice—

Wait. These are no angels. Henry and Beatrice are hugging me. Rae stands over me with a flashlight.

I jolt to a seated position.

"Petunia!" I say. "Where is she?"

"*Petunia?*" Rae says. "*What are you talking about?*"

"She was here. Right here. Telling me to wake up."

"Petunia is dead," Henry says, so matter-of-factly that he seems like some especially rude kind of alien.

"Edie, that was me," Rae says. "*I* was telling you to wake up."

I blink and try to make sense of everything.

"Edith," Beatrice says, "you know you fainted, right? And fell into the water?"

"I found your glasses," Henry says, slipping them onto my face. "And Rae pulled you out."

"You did?" I look at Rae. I still feel a little spacey.

"Well, yeah," she says.

"Wow . . . *thank you*," I say. Then the memory of everything feels like a cyclone, hitting me all at once. "Wait! There was an alligator! What—"

"It's over there," Rae says.

I start to scramble, trying to stand up.

"No, don't." Rae gently pushes me back down. "It's a

little waterlogged, but it's not alive. Well, not anymore. It's stuffed."

"Like Odysseus," Beatrice says. "And Herbie."

"But it looked so *real*," I argue.

"That's the point of taxidermy," Henry says.

"And the water was moving, Edie," Rae says. "No wonder it looked real."

"Well, how'd you know it *wasn't*?" I ask Rae.

"It was turning belly up in the water when I got out here."

"Oh." So it was *rolling over*, not preparing for a predatory attack. I feel pretty stupid, although . . . "What was it doing in the swamp in the first place?"

"I don't know. It was all so crazy, Edie. Wait till we tell Mitchell about this!"

Mitchell. Hearing his name triggers a sinking feeling in my gut. I remember that Mitchell is her secret boyfriend. That my night was wrecked and ruined, just because she wanted to hang out with him—wait, probably *make* out with him. *Gross.*

Then another thought pops into my head. *Item eight. Hug the person you least want to.*

She's standing right there.

After a whole summer of trying, here's an easy checkmark in the box. Rae's within arm's reach; I could just give her a quick hug, and check it off right now. But I can't bring myself to do it.

There's the sound of a siren in the distance. "Oh my god," Rae says. "I bet that's for us. Our parents must have discovered us missing and called Officer Elwayne. I'm sure we're really going to be in a whole *carp*load of trouble this time."

"I don't care," I say. "I just want to go home."

"Okay, let's go home," Rae says, offering her hands to help pull me up.

"No." I push myself to standing. "Home *home*. Not Petunia's place. *Home*."

I start walking. Beatrice catches up to me and grabs my hand. "It's okay, Edith. Summer's almost over."

Which is good, because I'm definitely over *it*. But I keep my mouth closed.

Beatrice holds my hand tighter, and we walk back together.

The house is lit up. Through the windows, we can see our parents moving around inside like outraged ants whose stash of crumbs has been stolen away. We hear loud and panicked voices before we even reach the porch. My mom is shouting at Uncle A.J. "Why is it that you're never in charge of them?"

"*I'm* supposed to be in charge? Since when did you ever trust *me* to be in charge of anything?" Uncle A.J. shouts back.

I'm the first one inside. Our parents seem to talk all at once when they see us; their words come out in a big jumble.

"Elwayne, *they're here!*" my dad says into the phone, his voice full of relief.

"What happened?" Uncle A.J. booms.

"Where *were* you?" My mom is frantic.

Their words crash into each other, so it's not clear how to answer or who to address first.

I expect the twins to jump in with some sort of breathless recap, but no one speaks, not even Rae.

"Edith?" my mom prompts, her voice impatient.

"I was trying to cross the swamp. It was our last full moon and—" I realize how ridiculous it sounds and stop myself. "You know what? I know it was stupid, okay? It was a bad idea, and I shouldn't have done it."

I am speaking should language. My mom's language. But she's not happy. "I have had enough of this, young lady! Do you hear me? Just enough!"

"Mom? I know. I get it." I might as well wave the white flag. For once, she was right. It was really dangerous. Really unsafe. "You may or may not believe me, but this is the last time that'll ever happen. I can promise you that."

"Well," my mom says stiffly. She looks hard and tough, like she's about to hand down a superstrict punishment. "*Well,*" she says again, and her voice sounds tight, like it might snap. And then it sort of does—*she* does. She starts crying. It bursts out of her, like it's been waiting there for a long time.

After a few moments—my dad and A.J. exchanging worried looks—she finally sniffs and wipes her face with a tissue. She looks back up at us all and says, "Is anyone hurt?"

"I got a splinter," Beatrice says.

"Let me take a look," my dad says.

"And I got a scrape on my elbow," Henry adds.

"Let's get that cleaned out," my dad says.

"How about you two?" Uncle A.J. asks Rae and me. "You okay?"

Rae, of course, has managed to get by without even a bruise. I just nod. No visible scars, at least.

My dad and Uncle A.J. start tending to the twins' wounds, and I say, "Mom? What's our punishment?"

She gives me an odd look, like she's not really sure who I am. I'm not really sure either. I do feel different.

"I mean, just tell me what it is, okay? I'm not going to argue, I just want to know what I'm dealing with."

She sighs. "Edith, I'm too tired to even think right now."

"Yeah, I think we all are," Uncle A.J. says. "For now, let's just be glad that everyone's okay. Let's just be glad that we're all home, and we're all safe."

My mom flashes him an appreciative glance. "I'm sorry I yelled at you. I do trust you."

"I know. And I'm sorry I can be such a jerk sometimes," Uncle A.J. says.

"Tea, anyone?" my dad offers. I know he's just dying to use his new electric kettle.

"Thanks, Walter. I'll have some."

Uncle A.J. says he will too.

After the wounds are fixed and bandaged, Beatrice finally starts pouring out the details—leaving out the fact that they were out there filming in the first place—and then the parents send us all off to bed. On our way upstairs, I hear my dad's sunshine-and-rainbows voice. "Well, how about that? We took a united front, and everyone's A-okay! Good work, home fries. Let's bring it on in! Come in here!" I glance over the banister to see my dad trying to huddle everyone together.

"Walter, my glasses are caught on yours," my mom says. She's not a fan of the group hug.

Apparently, that runs in the family. My uncle wheezes out a strained "Not so tight, bro."

But my dad continues to squeeze away.

"Wow, what's up with our parents?" Rae says when we get to our room. "I mean, did you see that? A group hug!"

"Yeah, I guess so." I'm still sort of reeling from everything that happened tonight.

"Maybe we should have scared them to death earlier this summer."

"Maybe."

I can feel her looking me at again, but I don't look back. "So," she says. "I can't believe you fainted. You must have been terrified."

My answer is cool. "Yeah, well, I thought the twins were about to get eaten. So, yeah—I think anyone would have been."

"True."

I sigh. As annoyed as I am with her, I say it again. "Thanks for pulling me out."

"You're welcome. Sorry I wasn't there earlier, you know . . ."

I wait for her to say more, but she doesn't.

So I ask the loaded question. "How *was* your month-iversary call?"

"Uh . . ."

I wait again, feeling ready to pounce.

"Not that great, actually." She looks away.

I make a *hmm-hmm* sound, which she seems to mistake for interest rather than skepticism. She must not know that I heard her over at Mitchell's. She must think I'm oblivious. That I'm stupid. Boring and stupid.

"I mean, it's tough being away from each other. Really tough." She shakes her head. "I don't know. Sometimes I think we're like star-crossed lovers."

"*Aaaaand*, cut," I say.

Her head jerks in my direction, her face a big question mark.

"I mean, at some point you have to break for a commercial," I say.

She stares at me.

"Intermission?"

Her left eye narrows a little.

"Why are you acting like this, Edie?"

"*Acting?* Am *I* acting? No," I say. "I think not. In fact, you're the actor—you've been the star of the show this whole summer. Tonight was no exception. But you know what, Rae? At some point, the curtain's got to close."

"Oh. So you *did* know I was at Mitchell's, then."

"Uh, yep. I definitely did."

"Okay, first, you have to know that it's not what it looked like—"

I almost laugh. "It's not what it looked like." That's such a well-worn line in any cheesy television show. So maybe it shouldn't surprise me that it's coming from her.

But she's stopped talking.

"Well, what was it, then?"

"I needed a friend, Edie, and—"

"A friend who you just secretly hang out with?"

"I wasn't trying to be sneaky—"

"And watch movies with—"

"Come on, Edie."

"And make out with—"

"What? *Edith!*"

Hearing her call me by my real name jars me.

She continues, "I'm trying to talk to you and you're not listening!"

I stare—no, *glare*—at her, challenging her to explain.

"It's not at *all* what you think."

"Rae, most of the time it doesn't really feel like you even care what I think!"

"I *do* care what you think. I care *a lot.*"

I feel like a dam has broken—like I can't stop my thoughts from being spoken. I blurt, "Yeah, maybe you care about what I think about your acting. Or your jokes. Or about all your performances, sure. But if it's not *you you you*, it's meaningless, isn't it?"

I suck in a breath, surprised at the sharpness of my own words.

"Good night," she says sharply, and rolls away.

But then I hear quiet, mouselike gasping sounds and I realize she is crying.

All summer long, I've wanted to be more like her—fearless, brave, bold, adventurous. I've lied, I've broken rules, I've worked so hard at it, and I've failed *epically.* And now this is what I have to show for it—she's quietly sobbing, and I'm starting to feeling like a toad. No, wait, a toad is too nice. A snake.

"Sorry," I murmur. It's the only thing left in my try-hard toolbox. "I saw you there, and I guess . . . fine, just tell me."

She sniffles and then gets quiet.

"Rae? I'm listening, okay?"

She finally speaks. Or rather, she seethes. "I *said* good night."

I roll over, away from her. And I attempt to sleep, as if effort has any role in it. I guess sleep is a lot like friendship. The harder you try, the more it escapes you.

Chapter 24

Good Ideas for Summertime, Revised

The next morning, I'm practically still awake. The twins come in, ready to sneak attack me, but Beatrice notices my open eyes. "Oh." She seems surprised. "You're not asleep."

"Nope."

"Well, why are you guys just lying there?" Henry asks.

I wonder if Rae's awake, and if so, for how long she's been.

"No good reason," I say.

"Are you sad about last night?" Beatrice asks. "About being in trouble?"

"Sad? No, I'm not *sad*."

"You seem sad about *something*."

I give her a little smile. Guess she is kind of cute sometimes. So earnest.

"You can come with us today if you want," Henry says. "Dad says we're going to look for the grasshopper sparrow."

"You gave up on the scrub jay, too?"

"He shrugs. Come on, Edith, we're leaving soon."

"Thanks, Henry, but I don't think I'd be any fun. Go on downstairs now, though, okay?"

Surprisingly, they do, without any arguing or further questioning. Even they can tell things are off.

When the door closes, Rae sits up. She has this sort of resigned look on her face. "So, what about the list? I thought you wanted to finish it," she says in this tired, worn way.

"I don't know," I say. I want to make up with her, but I still feel left out. Betrayed.

And unsure of how to fix things.

"Yeah, me either." She sighs.

The hurt part of me keeps talking. "Well, you probably crossed the last thing off the list last night anyway," I say. *"Kiss the charmer."*

"Oh, come on, Edith, I did *not*," she says.

So I guess Edith is sticking. It feels like the dynamic duo has disappeared into thin air.

So I say, "I guess we just forget about the list. Who knows what any of it meant anyway? Seems like a wild goose chase."

I watch for her reaction, hoping to see some sort of sign that she cares. But her face is still. I try one more thing. "I mean, if we're honest, the whole summer has probably been one long wild goose chase."

I actually want her to argue with me, to tell me I'm wrong. That if nothing else has worked out, at least we've had each other. But she just says, very coolly, "Agreed. A lost cause."

Despite the weight of disappointment, I add, "Maybe we should just focus on getting out of here. If we actually work on the house instead of trying not to all the time, the sooner it'll be ready to sell, and the sooner we can all go home."

She looks right at me. And says, "That's the best idea I've heard all summer."

"Hey, sport!" A.J. calls up the stairs. "Coffee?"

"Definitely!" she calls back. Then to me, she says, "Well, I'm going downstairs."

"Enjoy your coffee," I say, very civilly.

"Yeah, thanks. Enjoy your *whatever*," she says, just as civilly, back.

I take my time getting up and dressed. I have a tiny glimmer of hope that maybe, just maybe, she'll bound back up the stairs, breathless with regret. That she'll tell me that she can't stand this; that she needs me as her friend. That we have to make up. That she wants to finish what we started. That we're in this together. Whatever this *is* anymore.

But I realize the best I'd get is some movie quote—or worse, Shakespeare—that I wouldn't understand.

At nine o'clock, I give up and go downstairs. I sip my coffee (creamed, sugared, and spiced), and look around the quiet kitchen. Despite my dark mood, I have to admit that the ivory-painted cabinets really do brighten up the place. The new appliances really do "bring the kitchen into the twenty-first century," as my dad promised they would. Still, I'm a little annoyed at its cheerful elegance, until I realize that it means we're closer to going home.

Which is what I want.

At ten o'clock, I'm finishing my second cup of coffee, and Rae is still nowhere around. Whatever. Rae's no doubt charming Uncle A.J. into not punishing her for last night. Or maybe she's back at Mitchell's. Making cookies. No, forget that. Making *out*.

My mom walks into the kitchen. "There you are. How are you feeling this morning?"

I shrug. "Weird, I guess."

She sighs and looks at me. I have a feeling she's about ready to launch into a long and unnecessary safety lecture. So I ask, "So what's our punishment?"

"I don't know, Edith. I just think—well, I want you to decide that."

"Me?"

"Yes, Edith. You already know my rules, and you're old enough to know right from wrong. You decide."

I hear the door open, finally. Rae and her dad chatting breezily. Like her dad is suddenly her best friend. They walk into the kitchen and see us. "Oh, *hi, Aunt Hannah!*" Rae says, as if she's in a musical. I can see her smiling, spinning, singing, *the hills are alive!*

"That was. The best coffee. *Ever*," Rae continues. "We went to the diner."

"This kid actually taught Dani how to make it a little better."

Of course she did. She probably got a standing ovation.

"Mom," I say, now more eager to get out of this summer than ever before, "will you please give us a list of everything that still needs to be done for the house? As many things as you can think of? As our punishment."

"Yeah, Aunt Hannah," Rae says, in her spotlight-smile way. "That would be great."

My mom's mouth opens a little. She looks from Rae to me. "A to-do list? Sure, I can do that if that's what you want. But listen, I don't want to be chasing you two down."

"Oh, you don't have to worry about that." Rae's words are directed to my mom, but they're definitely meant for me.

"What's gotten into you two?" my mom asks.

"Well, I'm just ready to get home," I tell her. "The sooner

we can get this place ready to sell, the better."

"Amen to *that*," Rae says.

My mom looks surprised, but Uncle A.J. says, "I can't believe it's almost over. I know it's been a lot of work, but it's—just look around. This place looks better than it ever did."

"Well, I have to hand it to you, A.J. You put in a lot of work."

"Right back at you, Hannah. And I have to admit, Walt's got a knack for making things look good, don't you think? I kind of love this kitchen—it looks pretty awesome in here."

What's this? The new dynamic duo? I see a look pass between our two parents. One of commonality, of sharing the same kind of experience at the very same moment. A shared challenge, a common glint of pride.

I miss those looks myself—between me and Rae. I mean, up until lately it's felt like the Summer of Us. But in reality, it's been the Summer of Her, her, *her*.

With a tightness in my throat, I think about Petunia's now-abandoned list. I swallow it down. I don't want to feel sad. I will *not* feel sad. I'm not the pathetic, please-like-me girl I used to be, and I am grateful for that. Hear me? Grateful.

I look up and see Rae staring at me. It shakes my resolve a bit. But whatever.

Just because she can't be a great friend doesn't mean that she can't be a good coworker.

Chapter 25

So Charmed

There's no talk of the good ideas list anymore. That's been replaced by the to-do list. For the past week, we've been painting window trimmings, sorting the last of Petunia's clothing, cleaning up paint stains, Q-tipping between baseboards and floorboards, and now we're clearing out the closet beneath the stairs.

It smells like mothballs and something else—that smarmy-sweet aroma of decay. Or, if you're Rae, it just "reeks."

"Yes, it does," I say. "But in a couple weeks, this will all be just a memory."

She sweeps a hand in the air and starts. "Time—thou

ceaseless lackey to eternity."

Guess *I'll* be doing the heavy lifting. I take a box off the top of a two-tiered stack. It's full of books, and heavy enough to make me topple a little as I set it down to sort.

"Careful!" she says. *So* helpful.

She points to the one box left. It's folded closed, with its corners tucked under each other. On the side of the box, in Petunia's handwriting, are the words PAST/PRESENT.

"So that's where I get my amazing organizational skills," Rae jokes.

It's something I want to laugh at—would laugh at, if things were right between us. But now, I don't dare offer her more than a polite smile.

She pulls it over in front of her and sits down. "I'll go through it."

"Wait . . . ," I say. I kind of imagined we'd do this together. Sort through the last boxes of Petunia's things and reminisce, somehow, over our grandmother's life. Our common denominator.

She looks up at me. "What?"

I almost suggest it. But I remind myself that none of this matters very much anyway. We're just trying to get out of here.

"Never mind." I might as well face it. On Thursday morning, bright and early, a huge, groaning trash truck will chew up a large chunk of our family history like it's a piece of beef jerky. And the world will still keep spinning. Life will still amble on.

She opens the box and begins to go through it. Fast. Pulling out receipts and old papers and then—

"Oooh, what's this?" Rae says, taking out a photo and studying it.

I try not to seem too interested.

"Oh my god, he's going to *love* this," Rae gasps in her crave-the-spotlight way.

Still, I can't help myself. "Who's going to love what?"

She hands it over to me. It's a photo of Petunia, surrounded by a small group of kids—one of them Mitchell. He looks a couple years younger than he is now.

"Well, maybe you should give it to him, then." I try to pass the photo back to her, but she won't take it.

"Actually, I think *you* should," she says.

"Why should *I*? He's *your* friend."

"Edie, just stop, okay? You're the one he likes like that."

"Well, whatever, I don't like him back."

She shakes her head. "I can't believe a word that comes out your mouth, can I?"

"Is this about Klaus? I told you I was sorry. And I meant it. I still do."

She shakes her head. "You're just like the rest of them."

"The rest of *who*?" I ask, feeling sincerely puzzled. "All your besties? All your friends?"

"I don't have many friends."

"What are you talking about? You have all sorts of friends."

"No, I don't, not really. I have people who sometimes hang out with me, but mostly because they need a crowd. Or maybe they like something I put on Instagram, because it's super easy to do, and they know if they like my stuff, I have to like theirs. But it's not like they're real friends, like we were."

Past tense.

"Rae, I wish I could take the whole Klaus thing back. It was stupid."

"Yeah, it was," she says bluntly. "But it's not just about that."

"If it's about Mitchell, you're the one who—"

"It's not really about him either. Or the snakes—"

"I didn't really lie to you about the snakes, Rae. I just didn't really tell you how scared of them I really was."

"But that day in the shed, I gave you a chance to tell me why you don't trust me with, oh, anything, and you started talking about a trip to the zoo when you were six!"

So when she had said, "I don't always understand you," she meant she didn't understand why I just didn't trust her with these things. She wasn't looking for the history of my snake issues!

I do feel bad, I do. But—

"I'm really sorry about not always telling the truth," I say. "I really am. But haven't you told me some lies this summer too?"

She looks at me, puzzled. "Me? No."

Wait. What? I thought we were getting somewhere here. I'd confess, she'd confess, and maybe we'd be friends again. "But—I still don't really understand what you were doing over at Mitchell's that night."

"Yeah, I tried to tell you and you wouldn't listen!" Her voice is full of frustration. "All summer long you've been like that!"

"Rae, I *try* to listen! I *try* to be your friend, but sometimes it's hard because—" I stop myself. I start to fidget with a jagged fingernail.

"What, Edie?"

"I don't know, Rae, sometimes . . ."

"Sometimes *what*?"

My pulse is racing. It's becoming harder to breathe.

"Edie, please. Just tell me."

And then I realize why I'm so incredibly scared. Even with all the adventuring, and sneaking, and snaking, and whatever, this may be the scariest thing I've done all summer. I'm finally about to speak the truth—and apparently, telling the truth takes a whole lot of guts. Which I have, I remind myself. Who knows? I've probably grown an extra spleen over the summer.

Her eyes are wide open, like she wants to hear what I might say. And I know that maybe she needs to hear it.

I sit down on the floor near her. I center myself. Or at least I think I do. I take a breath. Three counts in, four counts out.

"Well, sometimes . . ." I need to choose my words carefully. "Not always, but sometimes . . ."

She nods, still looking at me.

"Sometimes it feels like you just want an audience, not a friend."

"What do you mean?"

"All the movie quotes and Shakespeare—I mean, that's great for performing. But I want to know things are real. That they're not just part of an act."

"But they're not an act!" she says. "When I quote from something, it's still real! It just means that someone said it better somewhere. It's still what I believe."

"I like it better when you just *say* what you believe."

"It's just that—" She stops for a second and looks at me. "I always feel like I have to say the right thing. Like if I don't, people won't, you know, like me."

"Well, that's why I made up Klaus," I say. "I just thought you'd, you know, think I was cool. Or more like you, at least. And you'd want to hang out—and do the list with me."

"His name was Klaus!"

"Yeah, uh, bad choice," I say. "At least Leo is real."

She's quiet.

"Wait. He is, right?"

"He's *real*," she says, pulling her knees in closer. "But he's not my boyfriend. Not anymore. He broke up with me."

"What? When? Why didn't you tell me?"

"I kept trying to, but you just weren't listening."

Memories appear like snapshots in my mind: the day I couldn't find her, because she was in the shed trying to reach him; the time she quoted Leo via Shakespeare—"'tis better to be brief than tedious." He'd been avoiding her; she sensed that it was going to happen.

"You know how Leo wanted to FaceTime me? The night of Corkscrew Swamp?"

"Your month-iversary," I say.

"Yeah," she says, a little sheepishly. "I thought he was going to apologize for avoiding me, but you know why he wanted to FaceTime? He didn't want to apologize—he wanted to dump me! It took about five minutes for him to put an end to the last six months. Happy month-iversary to me," she jokes.

I wince. "I'm sorry. I wish I had been paying more attention."

"Well, the whole thing pretty much sucked, and I didn't

really feel like I could come back and talk to you. So I went over Mitchell's and we just hung out and watched a movie, and he made cookies. He really can be a good friend."

I realize she's right. I've seen how kind Mitchell is—taking care of his little brother, being a good sport when Henry and Beatrice attack him with trivia. Offering me his sweatshirt that night we stayed out and watched the stars. It makes sense that he'd want to be a good friend to Rae that night, and I'm starting to feel really stupid that I wasn't a better one.

"Rae, I'm sorry. I'm really sorry. About everything. About Klaus. About lying. And I'm sorry about Leo too."

"Yeah, I think deep down I knew he didn't really like me like that. I might have forced the whole boyfriend role on him in the first place. I just didn't want to admit it. He's another drama geek like me . . . and you know, this whole time, I think he was just playing the part."

"Playing the part? But you've kissed him!" I remember all that weird pillow and vacuum talk from the beginning of summer. "Haven't you?"

"Only onstage. And you know what he does when we have to kiss? He starts counting on his fingers—one, two, three. And his face is all scrunched up like he's in pain. It's horrible, Edie. *Terrible.*" She sighs. "Well, I guess I see your point then. I do some performing."

I take a deep breath. "No, you know what? I guess I did

some performing myself this summer."

"Maybe we both did," she says. We look at each other and smile at the same time. I think back to when I first saw her—how it seemed like we were so different, despite sharing some common genes. It feels like I've finally found that mysterious twelve and a half percent.

And she seems to have found it too. "Edie, it just hit me. Like, *really* hit me. We're related. We're going to know each other for the rest of our lives."

I wonder if that's why Petunia made it a requirement in her will that we all come down and work on the house together. To somehow bring together in her death what she couldn't in life.

"So let's make a pact. From here until forever," she says. "No more pretending, no more performances."

"Deal," I say. "Except there's one more thing I need to tell you."

"What?"

"You know how you kept asking why the list meant so much to me?"

"Yeah?"

"Well, here's the thing. I've wanted to do the things on the list so I could prove to my best friend, Taylor, that I'm not a boring, no-fun scaredy-cat." I give her a half smile. "So she wouldn't ditch me for this new friend."

She looks surprised. "*That's* why you wanted to do the list?"

"Yeah. But so much for that. I didn't actually accomplish a single thing."

"But you did. And anyway, you're not a no-fun scaredy-cat. And you're not boring."

It's not exactly the ringing endorsement I'd have wanted. *Meet Edith! She's not boring! And she's not no-fun!*

"Well, I haven't caught a snake."

"Frogs are much harder to catch, trust me."

"And we never did find any hidden treasure."

"But we found a bunch of other things instead. Hoof-flavored ice cream! And toothpick trucks. And a stuffed alligator. Come on, Edie. Forget gold. This stuff is priceless!"

I smile. "And I never *actually* danced in the Hurricane."

"You can't possibly be a scaredy-cat and still break into an abandoned building in the middle of the night!"

"Well, okay. Maybe you're right. But I never mastered flirting. I failed that pretty badly."

"But you still somehow managed to ask a boy out—that night you saw the stars. And because you're such a bad flirter, that's an even bigger win! How exactly did you do that, anyway?"

"I, uh . . . have no clue. But I never saw a shooting star, so I couldn't make a wish on one."

"Doesn't matter. Science has proved that wishes on shooting stars don't come true any more often than wishes on your average nightly star," she says.

"Thank you, *Henry*." I laugh. "And I never actually wrote something scary."

"Well, I know you wrote something."

"Yeah, I wrote the real-life story about the zoo, but when I did, I realized it wasn't all that scary anymore. Like, this whole time, it's been taking up way too much room in my mind. And when I got it out, it just seemed a little ridiculous."

She smiles at me—the kind of smile that only a good friend could give. I start to feel a little melty, but I clear my throat. "And you know how Corkscrew Swamp went."

"Tragically," she agrees.

"Oh, and hug the person you least want to? You know, I thought about it that night, and I didn't hug you *on purpose*. I was too mad."

"You can hug me now, if you want," she says.

"Yeah, but now, I actually sort of *want* to hug you, so it doesn't even count."

She leans forward and wraps her arms around me. I laugh again, and hug her back.

"Anyway, it doesn't matter what you didn't do this summer, Edie. You *are* brave. And you're going to do something else pretty gutsy now."

"I am?" I ask.

"Yep. Go give Mitchell this photo. Go see him."

She slips it into my hand. I look at the picture again. It's sweet.

I hesitate. "Will you come with me?"

"Nope."

"But what about the dynamic duo?" I ask.

"We'll *always* be the dynamic duo, but you've got to do this on your own."

Maybe it's her certainty that convinces me. And that little trill of nervousness I feel—I realize that may never go away. Maybe it's just one small part of being brave.

Then she says, "Oh, Edie, there's one thing left on the list that you haven't tried yet, in case you really do want a checkmark."

That look alone tells me she's talking about item nine. Kiss the charmer.

"Right," I say.

The mischievous Rae smile is back.

Wait. "I mean that in a sarcastic way, not a 'you're right, I should do it' way."

She shakes her head. She laughs. "Just go."

I knock on the screen door, and it sets off Colvin. *Byebye-byebye.*

Mitchell appears on the other side of the screen. "Sorry, he's playing with his Legos and doesn't really want company," he says. "Let me get him settled and I'll be right back."

I take a seat on his porch steps and try to be calm despite the reminder that my heartbeat can get a little haywire around him, even though we're just buds.

The screen door screeches open behind me. He sits down next to me, and we look at each other. There is serious eye contact going on. He opens his mouth as if to declare something, maybe something important. His affection? His true regrets? And he says—

"*Testudinal* means looking like a tortoise shell."

Wait. My eyebrows crunch together. "*Testudinal?*"

"Yep." He shifts around a little and leans forward. "And a turtle shell is made up of sixty bones."

"Oh. Okay?"

"And a group of tortoises is called a creep."

"A *creep*?" I ask.

"Yep."

"Okay, then," I say. "You're acting like a group of tortoises then."

He gives me an almost smile.

"You said you wanted to talk about turtles," he says. "Last time I saw you."

Oh. Right. My wonderful ability to think on my feet. The

night I found Rae here with him.

"So I did some research. So we could talk."

"Okay, then," I say. "Let's talk. Because I've been wondering why you've been acting weird around me ever since the sea-stars night."

"Yeah, uh, about that," he says, stammering a little. "Well, uh, the next morning, when I was trying to tell you it was fun—"

"A good night," I say.

"Yeah . . ." He gets a little pink.

"What?"

"You—you laughed at me."

Ugh. When I snortled and chortled and made those awful involuntary laugh grunts.

"So that's why you called me your bud?"

"I thought that's what you wanted," he says. "You know, just to be friends."

"Oh, I do. I mean, I want to be friends, but not, like, buds, where we arm wrestle." What *am I saying?* "And, like, catch frogs, and—"

"You don't like the frogs?"

"No, I do, *I do.* I love the frogs. I mean, I like them. Let's keep catching frogs . . . uh." I make myself stop talking. And I take a big breath. "Mitchell, listen. That laugh . . . is just a thing that sometimes happens when I get nervous." And I finally say what I only wish I'd had the nerve to say a while ago. "Especially around someone I—I kind of like."

He starts to dimple. I smile and look away.

"Here," I say, dropping the photo in his lap. "It's a picture of you. And Petunia. And some kids."

He picks up the photo and studies it. I expect his face to light up, but it doesn't. He just says, "Cool. Thanks."

"Who *are* they?"

"Some friends. From my old school."

He's acting weird again—I decide to try a joke. You know, like Rae once said, give him a sort of hard time. "Well, it's good to know you have friends. The only other people I've seen you with are those kids in the Pinne Mafia."

But he doesn't really crack a smile. "Yeah, and those guys aren't my friends."

"I mean, I kind of figured. They don't even know your name. Weren't they calling you Ed that day we saw you with them?"

He stares straight ahead. "They weren't calling me Ed by mistake or anything. They were calling me Ed as in special ed."

"Oh" is about all I can manage, because I feel so stupid for another great flirt fail. Way to joke with him!

He glances over at me. "I used to go to a special school. Those kids in the picture, they were my classmates."

"So those guys that day—they were being jerks?"

He nods. "Try going to regular school after people like them find out you used to be in special ed."

I have a flashback to the night of stargazing, when he told me he went three years without talking. "Does this have anything to do with those three years you didn't talk?"

"Yep. Selective mutism. That's what it's called when you don't talk, even though you can," he says, and then jokes, "Although I didn't really *select* it."

I've heard about this. That sometimes young kids can develop this if something traumatic happens.

"A lot of people thought I was really weird. But not Petunia. She let me bring my classmates here. She taught us all how to handle the snakes. And it helped me. I started talking again."

I'm reminded of the conversation I had with Dani at the diner. "So snake therapy—it's a real thing?"

"Yeah," Mitchell says. "Snakes are really sensitive. They can sense if you're panicky, or nervous, or anxious, or anything."

I can sense a little of that in myself at this very moment. I guess maybe we could all use a snake sometimes.

I can't believe I just had that thought.

"I didn't want *you* to think I was weird, so I didn't tell you."

"Oh." I can understand that, but . . . "Well, I wouldn't have thought that just because you were in a special school."

"People say that, but . . ." He looks at me for a good minute with those blue-wait-no-green-no-aqua eyes. "You mean it really doesn't freak you out?"

"No. Not that. Plenty of other things about you do, but not that."

"Oh, yeah, like what?"

"Like—" I think about the first time I saw him. "The fact that you're a frog whisperer."

"Wow. Thanks."

"*And* a testudinal expert."

Wait. Am I flirting? Nope, because that's the worst line ever.

I look over at him. The way his eyes lock on mine seems to lighten the force of gravity in my body, somehow. My heart soars, my stomach lifts into my throat, and my mouth corners seem to be working on their own terms, smiling really stupidly, and—

Oh, no.

Snort. Chortle. *Snort. SNORT. CHORTLE.* It is just as horrifying as the first time. No, wait, it's worse than the first. It's louder, gruntier, and more incessant. I've never been so unhappy to laugh before.

"I'm . . . sorry," I manage to say. I worry if he might think

I'm laughing at him again.

But this time, he's looking at me altogether differently. He's smiling. He's taking this as a compliment. He gets it. He gets *me*. He's—oddly enough—flattered.

"Oh, here's another thing about turtles—something really crazy," he says. "The soft-shell turtle pees from its mouth."

"Oh, *ew*." I make a face, despite being pretty flattered myself. He's flirting!

And he may be an even worse flirter than me.

Chapter 26

Ten

The list of good ideas for summertime has been revived.

It was Rae's idea to add a tenth item to the list, the one that Petunia left blank. She's convinced that I can't end the summer without checking one item off the list. So . . .

Number ten. Celebrate.

That's something we can do, and better yet, we can do it together, all of us. It's an open house. A "remembering" party. A screening party. A bon voyage. There seems to be nothing that we're not celebrating.

On the night of the party, music fills up the old house.

Zachary Amos, neighbor-slash-Hurricane heartthrob, is playing a Beach Boys song on an accordion, and his wife, Melba, sings happily along. "Wouldn't it be nice if we were older . . ." Despite the fact that her voice is as smooth as an alligator's tail, the music makes an upbeat backdrop for the party.

I'm in the foyer with my mom and Beatrice when Welles Augustus and his ma arrive. They're holding a five-gallon tub of ice cream. "Thought I'd bring some refreshments," he says.

"Thank you, Welles." My mom smiles at him. "Looks delicious."

"A fresh batch of Surprise Me,'" his ma adds.

Beatrice makes a face. "What flavor is that?"

I brace myself. Artichoke heart's delight? Clouds of cauliflower? Dreamy dill?

"Vanilla bean," Welles says.

"Oh, good," Beatrice smiles. "I like vanilla."

But—

"That's vanilla-*slash*-bean," Welles explains. "Homemade mix of vanilla and baked beans. Ma even added some pork fat."

"Welles, that's the surprise part of the Surprise Me!" his ma scolds. Then she turns her head, as if just now hearing the music. "*Oh, my!* Is that an *accordion*?" She beams and clasps her hands in front of her chest—looking suddenly about twenty years younger before going off to find the source.

Over the music, I hear the ripping sounds of a car motor. It seems like it can't get any louder, until it does. A yellow Corvette parks in front of the house, and Dani jumps out of the car, her hands full of to-go boxes from the BEST Diner. She calls out, "I brought the fried pickles!"

"Oh, good—Hannah's favorite!" Uncle A.J. says as he comes down the stairs. He smirks in my mom's direction.

"Oh, A.J., Welles and his ma here just brought over a giant tub of vanilla bean ice cream. I don't know how we're going to eat it all. I think you should dive right in!"

His eyes widen. For a second, I can imagine my uncle as a ten-year-old. "Awesome," he says. "That sounds great. I could use some ice cream right now."

He goes down the hall into the kitchen. My mom and I look at each other and break into a big laugh.

Mitchell and Rae show up with a big plateful of cookies they made for the party. As we're putting them out on the reception table, Officer Elwayne's patrol car pulls up and he gets out. Rosie Dunwoody, the alligator trapper, steps out from the passenger's side.

"Oh, hi, Elwayne," my mom calls out to him. "Come on

in—we're just getting started."

"Thank you, Hannah," he says. "But first, some official business. This here's Rosie Dunwoody, our local gator wrangler."

"Uh, hello," my mom says, but she looks suddenly nervous. "What's going on?"

"Well, that evening all the kids ran off—I'm sure you remember," Officer Elwayne says.

The expression on my mother's face makes it clear that she remembers it all too well. Rae and I exchange an embarrassed look.

"It seems a few boys in town were pulling pranks with that gator all summer. All those alligator sightings? Those boys were behind every which one—planting Petunia's beloved old pet anywhere they could get a rise out of folks, then taking it away before we could catch them."

My mom's mouth falls open. *"Louis?"*

"That's right," Officer Elwayne says. "They must have stolen him from your property before you arrived. Seems their last and final prank was to try to float that stuffed alligator down the swamp."

The Pinne Mafia, I realize.

Officer Elwayne continues. "Found those boys that night you called looking for your kids." He nods at me and Rae.

"They hadn't gotten far."

"So . . . Louis? Well, what happened to him?" Mitchell seems concerned.

"Let's just say that those boys are working on their karma." Officer Elwayne smiles. "Took a little, shall we say, *encouragement*, but they decided to right their wrong. They've taken the gator to the taxidermist to get him restuffed. I hear he'll be good as new. Isn't that right, Rosie?"

"Like it never happened," she agrees.

My mom turns to Mitchell. "You knew Louis?"

"Well, not when he was alive, but Petunia gave him to me last year. She said it was good to have an alligator to look in the mouth sometimes. I'm not sure what she meant by that, though."

I think I do. I look at Rosie Dunwoody, and she smiles at me.

Officer Elwayne peeks past my uncle's shoulder. "Well, things sure do look good in there."

"Come in," Rae says. "I'll show you around."

My mom goes to check on something in the kitchen, leaving me alone in the foyer with Mitchell.

I look at him. "I can't believe those jerks stole Louis from you. It's so stupid. I mean, just because you went to a special school?"

"Yeah, it's stupid, but that's what guys like them do," Mitchell says. "They take stuff from kids they don't like. Pencil sharpeners, lunch money. *Alligators.*"

"But I still don't get it." I can't imagine anyone not liking him, so I blurt out a stupid question. "Why wouldn't they like you?"

As soon as I ask it, I know the answer. It doesn't always take a *why*. Some people are just looking for a *who*.

But Mitchell doesn't seem too fazed. "For being different, I guess."

And he sort of smiles at me, and I realize why I like him. Why I *really* like him. Because he *is* different, and different is starting to feel like a good thing.

I don't want the moment to end, but he tells me he needs to go feed the snakes. I start to go outside too—maybe the twins need help setting up their presentation. But on my way, I notice my mom standing at the newly installed kitchen island, just staring at nothing.

"Mom? You okay?"

She blinks, and then looks at me. "I was just thinking." She lets out a sigh-laugh. "Do you know what I just realized, Edith? I spent half my childhood being jealous of Louis, that poor toothless alligator. It feels pretty silly now."

Kind of like feeding time at the zoo, I bet. I smile. "So,

Mom, do you think that's why you've never let us get a pet?"

Her eyebrows lift. "Well, I don't know. Maybe so. I never thought about it like that." She seems to think about it now, though. "Maybe it's why I do a lot of things."

"Like have so many rules?" I ask.

She gives me a look. "Don't push it. It's only because I care."

"You know, I wouldn't mind if you cared a little bit less."

"*Edith,*" she says, but there's a little smile starting in the corner of her mouth. She leans back into the counter. "You know, honey, I'm kind of grateful that Petunia was the parent she was, even if she wasn't perfect."

"You are?" I ask.

"I am. Because if she had been a different parent to me, then maybe I would have been a different parent to *you*, and *you'd* be a different person." She rests her palms on the edge of the counter behind her. "And I wouldn't want to change that. I like who you are."

I look at her. *Really* look at her. And I start to see the blackberry-thicket free spirit, trying to stand out. I see the high school truant, trying to break out. I see the daughter, trying to avoid another falling-out. I see my mom, always on the lookout.

And I see the person, the sum of these parts, smiling at me now, trying to reach out. I realize that's what she's been trying to do all along, with all of her rules. She's been reaching out all my life.

This time, I reach back. And I give her a big, fat hug.

Outside, the twins' documentary is showing on the side of the freshly painted house. Though their mission was to capture an endangered bird on film, the video is a bit of a detour. After a fruitless search for Bachman's warbler, then the sparrow-tailed kite, then a Florida scrub jay, *then* the grasshopper sparrow, *then* an endangered *anything* of any kingdom, phylum, or class *whatsoever*, they resorted to filming any creature of any type that is rare, or even not so rare, alive or not so alive. As expected, the alive things are mostly running for their lives. Set to a pop beat, the film shows frogs, squirrels, snakes, Herbie, Albert/Odysseus, all sorts of common birds, and finally, Beatrice's elusive kitten, which was finally caught on film when Beatrice set the camera on a tripod in solitude all night.

"Oh, look, here's Aristotle!" Beatrice calls out. "Now everyone gets to see him!"

In the greenish night-vision tone, we can't quite make out the kitten's color. But we can see other things. Like his crooked tail. The dark markings on his ears and snout. A little cowlick on his back.

"Beatrice!" My father almost chokes on his lemonade. *"Puma! Concolor! Coryi!"*

"Puma concolor coryi?" Henry repeats, blinking.

"Puma concolor coryi!" Beatrice exclaims. Her eyes look almost as big as the lenses of the shared glasses.

"Excuse me," Rosie Dunwoody says, "I speak two languages—English and alligator—and I have no earthly idea what you're saying."

"Sorry about that, folks!" my dad says. "What we have here is the Florida panther."

There's some chirping and chattering among everyone watching, but Dani says, "The Florida panther? Can't be. There's less than a hundred of them left."

"You're right, Dani. Critically endangered." He turns to the twins. "Well, Beatrice, Henry, you should be proud of yourselves."

"But we didn't find any of the birds, Dad," Henry says.

"But this is magnificent—it's truly *wonderful*!" my dad says.

The twins just stare at him with matching expressions of confusion.

Henry says, "What do you mean, Dad? If this was an actual school project, we'd get an F."

But that doesn't seem to bother my dad. "Did you know," he says in a very twinlike tone, "that penicillin was discovered as a mold growing on the discarded petri dishes that Sir Alexander Fleming threw out, when he failed to find a 'wonder drug'? And do you realize that penicillin has saved hundreds of thousands of lives since?"

"Oh! I took that when I had an ear infection!" Beatrice says.

Rae turns to me and smiles. "One more thing to celebrate tonight. Epic failure."

I think of all the things that have happened this summer, despite the fact that I failed at all nine things on Petunia's list, and I smile. I'm already celebrating.

"No regrets, right, Edie?"

"No, but . . ." The moment feels right. "There is something from the list that I'd still like to do."

"What?"

"Um, it's probably best to do this with Mitchell."

"With Mitchell, huh?" A ridiculous, heavy-lidded look oozes onto her face, and she starts to make kissing noises. And *not* to scare off any snakes.

I get a little embarrassed. "*Rae*, uh—"

She laughs. "Go for it, Edie! And let me know how it is. It's *got* to be better than pillows and vacuums. The real thing, I mean."

I want to laugh, but there's no time. I'm ready for this now. "You want to come with me?"

"Uh, no. That would be"—and she sings the word—"*Awk. Ward!*"

I smile and start heading to the backyard. Into the dark. I feel great. Better than ever.

I can do this. I can do this! I can!

I keep walking until I'm there. At the snake enclosure. Right at the gate. And then past the gate. He's huddled over Imelda's cage but looks up at me. "Edie?"

"Hi," I say, feeling a little dizzy.

"Hi."

"So, Mitchell?"

"Yeah?"

In for three, out for four. "I need you for something—your help, I mean."

"Sure. What?"

Yes, he may be a charmer all right, but—

"Will you show me how to catch a snake?" My heart flutters around like that monarch butterfly. Emerging out of that cocoon of caterpillar soup. Ugh. *Thank you for that image, Henry.*

But Mitchell smiles. *Dimples.* And says, "Finally."

Chapter 27

Kingdom, Phylum, Class, Order, (Extended) Family

The minivan is packed. Very tightly. Very efficiently, like it's some sort of three-dimensional puzzle. It's just waiting for my family to get in and fill in the empty spaces.

Uncle A.J. gives me a soft punch to the shoulder. "Be careful out there, Spitfire."

I can't help but be flattered that he's calling me Spitfire now. I still wish it was Firecracker, but Spitfire will do.

Rae just rolls her eyes. I smile at my uncle.

Then I hear a voice cry out, "Hang on!"

I look over. Mitchell's running across the yard toward us, his wild hair springing out in all directions.

He's got something in his hands. A small cage. My stomach drops, my mind races.

What if it's a—

Just because I've actually held a snake in my hands doesn't mean I'm going to pull a Petunia and—

"I brought you all a turtle," he says.

Phew. And then my relief turns into excitement. A turtle! Something *testudinal*! This is our thing! We have a *thing*!

Henry holds out his arms. "Can I see it?"

"Oh. Sure. But leave him in the cage, okay? He's alive."

"Alive?" Henry and Beatrice say together.

"Yeah. Alive and moving. Not stuffed or anything," Mitchell tells them.

The twins wow and exclaim and practically swoon over the creature, which has tucked itself neatly—and smartly—inside its protective shell.

"*Wow.* A real pet!" Beatrice says.

"You can name him," Mitchell says. "He'll answer to anything."

I smile at Mitchell. Okay, I beam at him. I radiate. I'm practically radioactive with pure glee. He is cute. *Carp*, he's cute.

Rae nods at us. "Go say a real good-bye."

My face tightens with embarrassment. Mitchell turns a little red himself. My parents are talking over directions with my uncle, and the twins are arguing over names for the turtle.

Mitchell and I look at each other. "So, want to say bye to Imelda? You know, I think she kind of likes you."

I still feel a little shudder, remembering the strangely smooth feeling of the ball python sliding over my hand and forearm as I tried to breathe evenly. I tried to be calm. It's not that the fear went away. I just felt a little like I had outgrown it—like I had been trapped inside it for too long. I can't help but wonder if that's how a snake feels every time it sheds its skin.

Still, I'm not eager to do it again. Though I feel proud of myself, I'll admit that snakes are just not my thing. I wave in the direction of the enclosure. "Catch you later, Imelda."

Although I don't know when later will be, or if it will be at all. The thought makes me sad.

"Well," he says, looking a little splotchy.

"Well," I say.

Our eyes meet again. They're getting pretty good at that. And then I decide to go for it. Why not? Gutsy Edie isn't scared. Well, okay, maybe she is—but she won't let that stop her! I take a step closer to him, and he leans in toward me. I press my lips into his cheek, but he moves and the rim of my glasses shifts, and I'm suddenly staring into his ear.

Oh. I snort, and he laughs a little and wraps his arms around me. He squeezes me, a little too hard, and I squeeze back, a few extra seconds longer. Three seconds of my life I'll never, *ever* forget. Even though this hug feels sort of like the time I got stuck between the mattress and my wall, I feel strangely liberated. Oddly free.

We release each other. Our smiles seem to be stuck on our faces; I don't think I could make mine go away if I tried.

"Keep in touch, Edie, okay?"

I promise him that I will. We say our good-byes, and he walks off down the worn path. Halfway to his house, he turns and waves.

"So, how was it?" Rae asks, joining me.

"What?" I try to act casual.

"Kissing the charmer."

"Glorious failure," I say. "My glasses got stuck on his ear."

A laugh flies out of her.

I laugh too, although I suddenly want to cry. There's been talk about spending a holiday together, Rae's family and mine. *Our* family, I marvel. Ours with a capital O. But still, the summer's over, and I don't know for sure when I'll see her again.

"I wish we didn't have to go," I say.

"Me too. I'm going to miss you, Edie."

"I'm going to miss you too."

"I'm going to miss you more," she says.

"I'm going to miss you so much I could write a sonnet about it," I say, and it makes her laugh again.

We sit down on the porch step. She says, "It's weird to think I didn't even know you six weeks ago. Now I can't even imagine that. I feel so—"

She stops talking and shakes her head.

"What?"

"It sounds stupid. It doesn't even make sense."

"What doesn't?"

"How I feel. I mean, part of me just feels like *yay!* that I have you as a cousin. And a friend. But then the other part of me feels the exact opposite, since we're all going away. Like just the thought of us being apart—it actually *hurts*. It makes my heart feel super-scabby." She looks at me. "See what I mean? It doesn't make sense. Happy and sad at the same time."

"Rae, it makes perfect sense to me."

We smile together, but she looks like she's straining to keep something in. In fact, it looks like she'll burst if she keeps it inside for much longer. Even *I* know it's a prime opportunity to quote Shakespeare. So I just say, "Go ahead."

She straightens and adjusts the tone of her voice. "Good night, good night! Parting is such sweet sorrow." She adds, "Sorry, it's just that Shakespeare said it best."

I pull her into a hug. "Actually, Rae, *you* did."

Somewhere in Georgia, I get out a notebook and start making a list. Good ideas for the school year.

Talk to Rae every week.
Find something to do with Mom.
Make some more friends.

I stare at this last item, thinking of Taylor. Yesterday, when I took the last of the mail out of the mailbox, I found something wedged in the back corner. From the mid-July postmark, I could tell that it had been stuck there for a couple of weeks. It was a picture of the lake and trees at Camp Berrybrook. On the other side, just two words and some symbols.

Miss ya! XOXO—T.

It may sound strange, but the postcard made me think of a dinner we had last week. It was a busy night for the BEST Diner—so busy that Dani forgot to bring the fried pickles until after we had eaten dessert. We were still happy to get the pickles, but we were all pretty full. And pretty satisfied.

I continue writing.

Read some Shakespeare and try to understand it.
Ask parents for a real phone, not a Jitterbug.

It's Beatrice's turn with the glasses. She turns around in the seat and looks at me.

"What are you doing, Edith?"

"Making a list."

Paint my toenails glow-in-the-dark.

Because why not? Beatrice watches me write, and says, "Why do you want to paint your toenails glow-in-the-dark?"

I shrug. "Just for the fun of it."

Henry doesn't look up from his book, but he says, "That's a dumb idea. When Marie Curie discovered radium in 1898, it glowed in the dark too, and people started using it on everything, like their fingernails. And you know what? They died, Edith. *Died*. Someone finally figured out that it was poison."

"Here's a news flash for you. Henry," I say. "They don't make radioactive nail polish anymore."

"It's still pointless," Henry says, and turns back to his book.

"Oh, you know what?" I say. "I just got another idea for my list."

"What?" they both ask at the same time.

"Find a surgeon."

Henry looks up from his book. "Why do you want to find a surgeon?"

"Because you need a personality transplant," I joke.

Beatrice smiles. Henry does not.

"You can't *transplant* a personality."

"You're right, Henry. As usual, you're right."

Henry just sighs and shakes his head. "Edith, your list is full of bad ideas."

Bad ideas. I laugh. I add more to the list.

> *Write a love letter.*
> *Run away for a day.*
> *Ask someone to a dance.*

Let them be bad ideas. Ridiculous, irrational, pointless ideas. Because sometimes the worst ideas turn out to be the best ideas of all.

Acknowledgments

"I am not going to shy away from the things that make me uncomfortable sometimes."

It was a few years ago, at a very sad time, that I came across these words. I had just lost my mother to illness. I was cleaning out her house and found these words scribbled on the bottom of a household bill that I'd almost thrown out.

I don't know what was going on when she wrote those words, but finding this when I did felt especially significant. Grief had me wanting to shy away from everything, but these oddly placed "last words" made me think that maybe bravery comes in lots of forms.

We all have things that make us uncomfortable, or intimidate us, or even scare us witless—whether it's losing someone we love, or snakes, or mean people, or public speaking, or public restrooms. But maybe fear and growth go hand in hand. Avoid the things that scare you, and shrink—or face up to them, and grow.

These words became like a mantra to me. For that and much more, Mom, I'd like to thank you.

I'd also like to thank:

Joe McGrath for lots of much-needed love and encouragement, for the willingness to read and reread, and for mastering compassionate criticism.

Abby Ranger, my beloved and courageous editor, who led me to victory over such things as spy rings and secret weddings. If it sounds like I'm being melodramatic, trust me. I'm not.

Holly Root, my intrepid agent, who also happens to be a great problem solver and a motivational guru.

Kylie for sharp witticisms, Finn for intriguing insights, and Aidan for clever perspectives—and thanks to all of them for being so smart and funny, and for reminding me why I like writing for this age so much.

Michele Nesmith for always knowing how to put things in perspective for me. Meeting you in middle school was something I never stop being grateful for.

And if you're still reading this, thank you. May you find your own brand of bravery. And, of course, lots and lots of bad ideas.